ANIMAL
ALERT
RUNNING WILD

Animal Alert series

ANIMAL
ALERT

RUNNING WILD

Jenny Oldfield

Hodder
Children's
Books

a division of Hodder Headline plc

Special thanks to Julie Briggs of the RSPCA. Thanks also to
David Brown and Margaret Marks of Leeds RSPCA Animal
Home and Clinic, and to Raj Duggal MVSc, MRCVS and Louise
Kinvig BVMS, MRCVS

First published in Great Britain in 1998
by Hodder Children's Books

A Catalogue record for this book is available from the
British Library

ISBN 0 340 70876 X

Typeset by Avon Dataset Ltd, Bidford-on-Avon, Warks

Printed and bound in Great Britain by
Mackays of Chatham plc, Chatham, Kent

Hodder Children's Books
A division of Hodder Headline plc
338 Euston Road
London NW1 3BH

Foreword

Tess, my eight-year-old border collie, has been injured by a speeding car. I rush her to the vet's. The doors of the operating theatre swing open, a glimpse of bright lights and gleaming instrument, then, 'Don't worry, we'll do everything we can for her,' a kind nurse promises, shepherding me away . . .

Road traffic accidents, stray dogs, sad cases of cruelty and neglect: spend a day in any busy city surgery and watch the vets and nurses make their vital, split-second decisions. If, like me, you've ever owned or longed to own an animal, you'll admire as much as I do the work of these dedicated people. And you'll know from experience exactly what the owners in my *Animal Alert* stories are going through. Luckily for me, Tess came safely through her operation, but endings aren't always so happy . . .

Jenny Oldfield
19 March 1997

1

'Female Dalmatian, eighteen months old, having difficulty breathing!' Bupinda's voice came over the intercom describing an emergency admission to the vets on duty.

It was a Friday evening surgery in October. Carly Grey was carrying a stack of clean towels along a corridor in Beech Hill Rescue Centre. She stopped to listen to the receptionist's urgent message.

'Bring her in,' Liz Hutchins said, popping her head out of a treatment room door. The young vet slipped her stethoscope into the pocket of her white coat and reached for a pair of surgical gloves. 'Forget the laundry,' she told Carly. 'Stand by in case we need help.'

Carly dumped the towels on a nearby shelf and held the prep room door while their nurse, Mel, and the dog's owner carried the patient through. The large black-and-white spotted pedigree struggled feebly as they laid her on a treatment table.

Liz assessed the situation at a glance; the paddling legs, the dog's ribcage heaving in and out. She took a quick look at the blue colour of the tongue. 'Not good,' she murmured, telling Carly to move in and help restrain the panicking creature. 'What happened?' she asked the equally frightened owner.

'She was playing in the garden with the kids,' the woman gasped. She was dressed in a denim shirt and straight black trousers. Her dark, curly hair was tied back with a red patterned scarf. Shock made her gabble her words. 'I was busy in the kitchen so I didn't take much notice. Then Jack ran in to tell me Pippa couldn't breathe. At first I thought he was joking, then I went out and saw she'd collapsed. We jumped in the car and brought her straight here.'

'How long ago did this happen?' Liz had to consider what to do next. She tried to ease Pippa's jaws open, but stepped back quickly when the frightened dog jerked her head and snapped her sharp teeth.

'About twenty minutes ago. Do you know what's wrong with her?' The woman was close to tears.

'She's collapsed through lack of oxygen,' Liz explained. 'That's why her tongue's blue. I'm just not sure yet why it should have happened.'

'What game was she playing in the garden?' Carly asked. When the woman seemed too upset and confused to answer, she ran quickly from the prep room into reception. 'Is there someone called Jack here?' she said in a loud voice, across the waiting room full of owners queuing with their pets to see the two Beech Hill vets.

All heads turned towards her. A springer spaniel barked and strained at the lead.

'That's me!' A boy of about ten stood up. He

had the same dark, curly hair as his mother. His face was pale and scared.

'Jack, what game were you playing with Pippa when she got ill?' Carly asked. Seconds ticked by.

'Football,' he whispered.

She thought fast. 'How big was the ball? A proper football? A tennis-ball?'

The boy shook his head. 'Smaller; an old rubber one.'

Carly ran back to tell Liz. 'Pippa might have a ball jammed against her windpipe. That could be what's stopping her from breathing.'

'Thanks, Carly. Our main problem is that we should give her a general anaesthetic to allow us to move in and take a look. But her condition's too poor; her vital signs are weak. An anaesthetic would put a big strain on her heart. No, we'd better go for a local anaesthetic and hope she doesn't try to bite my hand off!'

'She's probably too weak,' Mel murmured, restraining the struggling Dalmatian's head as Liz eased the jaws open once more.

Pippa's blue tongue lolled out of her mouth,

4

her eyes closed as she fought for breath.

Carly watched Liz peer down the dog's throat.

'You were right, Carly. I can see the ball stuck down there as plain as can be.' Liz nodded and asked Mel to prepare an injection of local anaesthetic.

'Please hurry!' Pippa's owner pleaded. Every tick of the clock on the prep room wall could signal the poor dog's final seconds.

'Carly, pass me some large tweezers from the instrument tray,' Liz said calmly. She injected the drug into Pippa's neck and stroked her gently. 'Let's see if we can help you,' she soothed. 'You lie nice and still while we get this horrid thing out!'

Carly handed the vet the tweezers and watched her insert them between the dog's jaws. By this time, Pippa was so starved of oxygen she was almost unconscious.

'Hurry!' her owner urged, tears spilling over and trickling down her cheeks.

'I can feel it and I can see it, but I can't shift it!' Liz frowned and swung a light into a better position. 'The tweezers are no good, and my

5

hand's too big to get right down there!'

'Let me try!' Carly wasn't afraid that the dog would bite. She seemed to understand now through her haze of pain and fear that they were trying to help.

So Liz nodded and told her to put on a surgical glove. 'Have a go. Can you reach?'

Carly felt her fingertips make contact with the round object deep in the dog's throat. She nodded.

'Good. Now take a firm hold and pull.'

'Hard?' She felt her heart beat more rapidly. *This has got to work*! she told herself. *It's our only chance!*

'Yes, a good, firm pull. Ready?'

Carly nodded again. Gripping tight with her fingertips, she dislodged the ball.

'Got it?' Mel asked, holding on to the patient as her legs kicked and her head jerked back.

'Almost . . .' She felt the ball slip, then she tightened her grasp again. Slowly and gently now, she pulled the object out of the dog's mouth.

Pippa took her first clear breath. Her chest heaved, and there was a loud, rasping sound.

'Well done!' Liz told Carly. She turned quickly to Mel. 'Let's give her oxygen to help her get back to normal.'

The nurse strapped a plastic mask around the dog's face and Carly stepped back. She stared at the small blue ball. To think that something so ordinary could nearly cost a beautiful dog her life!

'No time to relax!' Paul Grey was as pleased as everyone else that Pippa's case had turned out well, but he knew they still had a waiting room full of patients to see. 'There's a budgie with scaly beak in treatment room 1. Would you like to take a look, Carly?'

'Scaly beak?' *Like, yeah*! she thought. Sometimes her dad's enthusiasm for his job was over-the-top, even for her.

'Come on, it's a really advanced case,' he insisted. 'A crusty coating caused by a mite. If you see it once, you'll recognise it in future.' Paul swung out of the door, expecting her to follow.

Carly sighed and braced herself. After a hard week at school and a weekend of homework ahead, a budgie with a crusty beak was exactly what she would enjoy.

Liz and Mel laughed at the look of disgust on her face. 'Go on!' the nurse encouraged. 'A vet's work isn't all dramatic rescues and saving lives, you know!'

Carly had to admit that if she wanted to follow in her dad's footsteps there would be a lot of routine work and uneventful illnesses to learn about, so she pulled herself together and went to join him.

He was in the treatment room hunched over the bird. He held it in one hand while he gently dabbed its beak with a cotton bud dipped in a special liquid that would kill the mites and cure the condition. The budgie was bright blue, with a grey-speckled head and grey wings.

'Found in the supermarket carpark, lying on his side under a bush,' Paul Grey reported. 'Probably been attacked by magpies and crows. If some kind soul hadn't spotted him and brought him in, he wouldn't have lasted the night!'

'Aah!' Suddenly Carly was interested.

'I wonder where he came from?'

'I guess we'll never know. It's practically impossible to trace the owners of escaped budgerigars unless they come here looking. And they hardly ever do.' He sighed, putting the groggy bird on to the floor of a clean cage.

'So what'll happen to him now?' She watched the budgie fluff out his blue chest feathers and huddle in the corner of the cage.

'He can stay with us for a day or two in the exotic pets section, until he gets over the trauma of being out in the big bad world. There's a Sun Conyer up there already, waiting to be rehomed.'

'Is that the green, orange and yellow one?' She remembered the pretty bird in the first floor room where they housed the 'exotics', which at Beech Hill meant anything that wasn't a cat or a dog! 'Then what?'

'I'll get Steve to drive them both over to Holybridge.'

The bird sanctuary was an hour's drive away, to the north of the city. 'Unless the owners contact us first,' Carly murmured, bending down to study the budgie. He had beautiful black markings around his throat and delicate speckles like a grey hood over his tiny head.

'They won't,' her dad said, as if it was a fact of life. He asked Carly to carry the cage upstairs.

When she came back down, still hoping that someone somewhere might be missing the blue budgie enough to come to Beech Hill and make inquiries, she walked into another crisis.

'Watch out!' a voice she recognised yelled through reception. It was her friend, Hoody. 'Get out of the way!' he insisted. No manners. No 'please' and 'thank you'.

'Which treatment room?' Steve Winter was asking Bupinda.

'Try number 1. Paul's in there. I think he's just finished with a patient.' The calm receptionist organised events as doors swung open and people in the waiting area muttered to Hoody about staying at the back of the queue.

'Yeah, yeah!' He couldn't care less what they thought. This was an emergency.

Carly saw his skinny back view as she reached the bottom of the stairs. He was already out of school uniform and dressed in his usual scruffy leather jacket. She ran to catch him up and look over his shoulder at a brown, black and white dog lying on the table, with her dad and the Beech Hill inspector, Steve Winter, bending over it. 'What happened?'

'Search me,' Hoody said angrily. 'I just found her lying there. And, luckily, Steve was passing in the van.'

'Lying where?'

'On that waste ground by the main road.'

'Past Hillman's?' Carly knew the patch off City Road where the bulldozers had moved in and flattened a row of terraced houses and shops. 'What was she doing there?'

Hoody didn't bother to reply.

'OK, stupid question.' She pushed past him into the room. At closer quarters she could see that the patient was some kind of hound; a beagle or a harrier. Her stocky body was covered in sores, her legs stuck out stiffly and the large ears, which should have flopped down against the sides of her head, were cocked at an angle.

'There's no doubt about it,' Carly's dad muttered. He watched the dog's head jerk back

11

in an uncontrollable spasm. 'This is a case of tetanus.'

'Lockjaw?' Steve frowned.

'Yes, you normally find it in horses. It's only the third or fourth time I've seen it in a dog. But there's no mistaking the symptoms.' He pointed to the rigid limbs and locked facial muscles. 'The poor creature can't eat or drink in this condition. No wonder she's collapsed.'

Carly drew near the table. The dog was suffering badly from the illness; in obvious pain and distress. 'How come she caught this?'

'It's most likely that one of these sores on her back has got infected. The germ responsible is called *clostridium tetani*. It's a hard one to beat.'

'Well, go ahead, what are you waiting for?' Hoody followed Carly into the room. He winced as he watched the dog's uncontrollable twitching.

'We need an antitoxin; a drug to beat the germ, which we don't keep here,' Paul explained. 'I'll have to send out to St Mark's Hospital for it.'

'I'll go in the van.' Steve made an instant decision. He took a signed form from Paul and headed off as fast as he could.

'So?' Hoody paced up and down the room, hardly able to look at the dog. 'What now?'

'We wait.' Carly's dad was honest, as always. 'Like I said, this is going to be a real battle, and it could go on for days if not weeks. She'll need constant nursing. She won't be able to stand, so we'll have to turn her every few hours to prevent bedsores.' He painted a bleak picture because he wanted Carly and Hoody to know what lay ahead. I've lost two of the dogs I've treated for tetanus in the past.'

'Can't we do something while we wait?' Carly too found it hard to watch. The twitching shook the dog from head to tail and the sores covering her body were dirty and infected. 'Can't we clean her up?' she pleaded.

Paul Grey nodded. 'And I can start her off on a dose of penicillin. She's going to need massive doses of antibiotics.'

'Go ahead!' Hoody said impatiently.

Carly helped hold the dog as still as she could while her dad found a vein in her front leg. 'What type is she?' she asked quietly, stroking her neck and watching a second needle being prepared to inject fluid. In under a minute, Paul had the patient hooked up to a drip via a long, plastic tube.

'She's a beagle; originally bred as a scent hound. Lovely, intelligent dogs.' He stood back and shook his head. 'This one isn't wearing a collar. I wonder why not.'

Carly turned to Hoody. 'Did you take one off?'

'Why should I?' He did his trick of answering a question with a question, more abrupt than ever.

She knew him well enough to know he wasn't really mad at her; it was because he was anxious about the dog. 'So we don't have a name or an address? But she must have cost a lot of money. Surely she's got a home somewhere.' She spoke her thoughts out loud, without expecting an answer this time.

The boy shrugged and backed out of the treatment room.

'Hoody!' She followed him and stopped him in the corridor. 'You're not holding something back from us, are you?' He said he'd found the beagle lying on waste ground, apparently

14

without a collar. 'Do you know who the owner is?'

He shook his head and set his mouth in a thin line, setting off towards reception.

'You do, don't you?' He was the sort who picked up everything that was going on on the streets around Beech Hill and City Road. She put a hand on his arm to stop him leaving. 'Come on, who owns this dog?'

He stopped and pulled his arm free. 'No one, OK?'

'What do you mean? You're saying she's a stray?' What proof did he have? He'd only just come across the dog lying on the waste ground.

Now he nodded. 'Right! No collar, no owner – get it? She's one of those dogs you see roaming about in the park and hanging about on the estates, scavenging food from the bins.'

'Running wild.' Carly knew the dogs; a big pack of them, half starved and homeless.

He nodded angrily. 'See? What I'm saying is, there's no one around to care if that dog in there lives or dies!'

Carly drew a deep breath and thought of the

battle ahead for the desperately sick animal. She looked Hoody in the eye. 'Except us,' she said quietly. '*We* care!'

2

'We'd better give her a blue card,' Bupinda decided early next morning. The beagle had made it through the night after her first injection of the drug from the hospital.

Carly had been to see her in intensive care and was now making out a ward card for the dog. They used green cards for owned pets, blue for strays. But over this one she hesitated. 'Are you sure?'

The receptionist flicked her long black plait behind her shoulder and looked up from the filing cabinet. 'She's a stray, isn't she?'

'It's not definite.' Carly pursed her lips stubbornly. She didn't want to give the beagle a number instead of a name. 'That's only what Hoody thinks.'

Bupinda scanned the case notes that lay open on the desk. 'No collar . . . cuts and scratches that make it look as if she's been in a fight . . . flea infestation. It all adds up to her not having an owner. What's the problem?'

Carly sighed and stared out across the waiting area at the brown leaves gusting across the Rescue Centre carpark. She saw Hoody coming through the gate with his dog, Vinny, shoulders hunched, hands thrust deep into his jacket pockets. 'Dad says her chances of recovery are only fifty-fifty.'

'Ah!' Bupinda closed the file. She saw Carly's dilemma. 'So, if they're sure there's no owner around, you think they might decide not to go on treating her?'

'Yeah?' Hoody loped in through the doors, bringing a blast of cold air. He'd caught the end of Bupinda's sentence. 'Do you mean the beagle? How come?'

'Because it'll be a lot of work to pull her through, and at the end of it all, even if she does survive, we still have the problem of trying to rehome her.' Carly confessed her worries to Hoody, who'd obviously come in to see how the dog he'd rescued was doing.

'What you really mean is, it'll cost too much to keep her alive!' he said scornfully.

'No!' She was stung. This wasn't the reason they might stop treating the dog. 'Honestly, Hoody, I meant what I said yesterday: I care about what happens to this dog. But I can see what Dad might say.' It was one of the most difficult decisions a vet in a rescue centre had to take. 'Think about it. If we can't find a new home for her, then in the end we'll have to put her down anyway!'

'A lot of wasted effort,' Bupinda confirmed, handing Carly a blue card to fill out. She sounded brisk and businesslike. 'Give her a code: STR22. Leave the owner's name and address blank.'

Slowly Carly began to write. 'STR22'. 'STR' stood for 'STRAY'. It was horrid that the sick dog should be without a name. She heard the office door behind her open.

'The Dalmatian made a complete recovery.' Liz was reporting to Paul Grey as they left the office. 'We didn't even need to keep her in. Thanks to Carly, I was able to send her home with a pair of very relieved owners.'

'What's this about stopping treating the beagle?' Hoody interrupted. He was immediately on their backs, wanting better reasons than Carly had given him.

'Who said anything about that?' Paul took a step back and frowned.

'No one.' Carly regretted speaking out. The very thing she didn't want to happen was now being argued over. She glared at Hoody to keep his mouth shut, then ducked her head, as if her mind was fixed on filling out the blue card.

'Still, it's a point,' Liz said quietly. 'We ought to consider what to do before we go any further.'

Paul sniffed and looked through his list of morning appointments. 'I *am* considering it,' he said quietly.

'What? You can't give up on her!' Hoody was

outraged. His eyes were fired up under his crop of dark-brown hair. 'You wouldn't stop treating some old tramp in hospital just because he was homeless!'

'It's not the same.' Carly's dad stayed calm. He stooped to pat Vinny, who had trotted up to greet him.

'It is.' Pacing up and down in front of the desk, Hoody muttered to himself. 'Exactly the same.'

'The fact that the beagle's a stray is only one issue. Another is that the poor dog is suffering a lot of pain and distress. She's sedated and on painkillers, but we shouldn't let her go on if we can't reasonably expect a cure.' Paul took time to explain patiently.

'Carly said it was fifty-fifty.' The boy stopped and listened.

'A bit better than that now that she's made it through the first twelve hours,' Carly's dad admitted. 'With the right nursing it's probably more like sixty-forty.'

'I'll help nurse her!' Carly came in eagerly. 'I'll stay in this weekend and concentrate on getting her better!' She knew how much difference it would make if the dog sensed that someone cared.

'Me too,' Hoody promised. Now that he saw a chink of hope, his mood swung round. 'And I reckon we should try to find her owner!'

Paul smiled briefly, then looked at Bupinda. 'We could do our usual checks around the other vets in the city, to see if anyone has reported a missing beagle.'

The receptionist nodded. 'It depends how long she's been lost. If it's recent, we stand a fairly good chance.'

'On the other hand, by the look of those sores and her general condition, she could have been a member of the pack that's running wild for some time,' Liz pointed out.

'In which case, we stand very little chance,' Paul confessed.

'Well?' Carly urged him to decide. The fate of STR22 hung in the balance.

Her dad weighed up the problem, studying Carly's earnest face beneath her mop of black, wavy hair. Her dark-brown eyes pleaded with him.

'OK, we carry on with the treatment,' he said at last.

'It's a fancy breed; a black lop.' Liz described the rabbit that had been brought in for treatment.

While Hoody was visiting the beagle stray in intensive care, Carly was helping at Saturday morning surgery as usual. She smiled at the docile, silky animal sitting on the table. Instead of standing upright like a normal rabbit's ears, the lop's flopped flat against his head, giving him a funny, droopy look. 'What's his name?' she asked the small girl who stood anxiously to one side with her mother.

'Dinky.' She held tight to her mum's hand and spoke in a frightened voice.

'It's OK, no need to worry,' Liz told the owners. She lifted one of the pet's comical ears and peered inside. 'Dinky has sore ears because there's a slight infection in there. It's called mange. I'll bet he's been shaking his head and scratching a lot, hasn't he?'

The fair-haired girl nodded.

'Well, to Dinky it must feel itchy and

uncomfortable, so I'm going to give your mum some powder to shake inside his ears and make it better.' Liz smiled at the little girl. 'While I'm here, I'll take a quick look at the rest of him.'

Carly watched her examine the rabbit's mouth and eyes, then run her hands over his shiny coat. This looked like a nice, straightforward case that would soon be dealt with. Glancing at her watch, she decided it was time to go and take over from Hoody in intensive care. But something the girl's mother had begun to explain to Liz made her stay.

'Usually we keep Dinky's hutch out in the garden, where he gets lots of fresh air, and he can use his run whenever he wants.' The woman took the rabbit from Liz and stroked him as she talked. 'But just lately those wild dogs have been sniffing around. They scare him half to death, so we've had to take his hutch into the garage.'

'Wild dogs?' Liz turned round from washing her hands at the sink.

'You know. This pack that roams around the estates and the park. Our garden backs on to the park, so they pester us a lot. I've rung the police about them, but I know they're too busy to do much. That's why I thought I'd mention it when I came here.' She sounded sorry to be a nuisance, but determined to get something done. 'They're definitely feral. Can't you round them up?'

'We can and we do,' Liz assured her. 'But it's not an easy problem to solve. Every time our inspector makes the time to bring a stray into Beech Hill, it seems there's another dog just waiting to take its place. The pack never seems to get any smaller, and meanwhile we have a struggle to find a home for the ones we've taken in.' She shook her head and shrugged. 'People don't want to take on animals that aren't house-trained. And quite a lot of these strays have other behaviour problems too.'

'But meanwhile there's a big bunch of them running wild in the park. I've talked to some other mothers I know, and we all feel it's only a matter of time before there's a serious accident.'

Carly looked from one to the other, and felt she could understand all sides of the argument. The mother's face had grown flushed beneath her straight, fair hair as she had her say. Liz had raised her eyebrows, as if to show that she understood but wasn't sure she could help.

'It's getting worse,' the woman insisted. 'People are afraid to take their own dogs for walks. And I certainly won't let my kids play in the park if I know the pack is anywhere near.'

Liz sighed. 'I'll speak to Steve Winter about it,' she promised. 'Out of interest, what's made it worse just lately?'

'There's one dog in particular.' Now that she'd started, the woman grew more and more heated. 'It's only recently joined the pack; probably about a week ago, and it's the one that really scares us.'

'What does it look like?' Liz showed she was willing to listen.

'You can't miss it. It's absolutely huge.' The woman held her hand above waist-height. 'Believe me, I'm not exaggerating. It's a giant of a dog!'

Carly frowned. Could this be true?

'As big as a Great Dane?' Liz prompted.

The woman nodded. 'The same kind of square head and long, thin tail. But stockier than a Great Dane. I think it must be a crossbreed, with some kind of mastiff in it as well.'

'No wonder people are scared,' Liz agreed.

'We think it's the leader of the pack. The others follow it because it's the strongest and fiercest. Whenever there's a fight, this is the one that wins.'

'That figures.' As the woman's voice rose and her little girl still clutched her hand, Liz spoke more softly. She gave Carly a worried frown. 'This is probably the one who the beagle was in a scrap with,' she muttered.

'And it seems to follow a set route. It hangs around the waste ground by the main road during the day.'

'That's where Hoody found STR22, isn't it?' Liz asked Carly.

Carly nodded.

'. . . Which means we feel relatively safe near the park, until about dusk, when it heads our way, bringing the rest of the pack with it. I tell you, it's scary when you realise it's about to get dark. You should hear the noise this giant dog makes when it arrives; a kind of weird howling.'

'Have you heard it?' Liz turned to Carly again.

'No. And I haven't seen it either. But I can ask Hoody.' Carly could rely on her friend to know more about this ferocious creature.

'It's like something out of a horror movie,' the woman insisted. 'You have the wind blowing and the night drawing in, the lights going on in the streets, then all of a sudden, this horrible sound of a dog whining and howling. It's so close it sounds as if it's actually in the garden. And if you catch sight of it, it's really dreadful. A huge creature stands in the moonlight, throws its enormous head back and opens its jaws to let out a blood-curdling cry. I tell you, it's terrifying.'

'OK.' Liz decided that this sounded urgent. 'I'll get Steve on to it straight away.'

'Oh, that would be great!' The woman sighed with relief. 'It would make all the difference. Without that great brute of a thing leading them, the rest of the pack might even split up and leave us in peace.'

'Steve's van's just driven into the carpark.' Through the open blind of the window behind Liz, Carly noticed the white van arrive.

'Tell him I'd like a word,' Liz told her, as she

opened the pet carrier for the woman to put the black rabbit back inside.

'. . . And don't worry, we'll do everything we can to solve the problem.' Carly heard Liz's reassuring voice as she went to find Steve.

But there was a picture in her head that she couldn't shake off. As she passed through reception and crossed the waiting area, she could almost hear the wind in the tall beech trees in the park, see the clouds drifting across the pale moon as it rose in the night sky.

She could imagine the giant dog leading the pack beside the quiet lake. He would be strong and fierce, his eyes would gleam in the moonlight as he threw back his head, opened his great jaws and uttered his wild, wolfish cry.

3

'She still can't stand up,' Hoody said quietly. He leaned against the white tiled wall, gazing at the beagle in the intensive care unit.

'No. It's too soon.' Carly reminded him what her dad had said: it could be a whole week before the anti-tetanus drug worked. But even she hadn't expected the dog to look so ill still. She lay on her side, legs stiff, a catheter needle strapped with white tape around her front paw. Her face muscles were rigid and the look in her dark-brown eyes as she stared back at Carly and

Hoody was a mixture of pain and puzzlement.

'She can't even drink, never mind eat.' Hoody shook his head.

'That's what the drip is for.' Carly moved forward to reach in and stroke the dog. 'Have you turned her over?'

Quickly Hoody shook his head. 'I was scared the tube might come loose.' The metal stands, plastic tubes, bright lights and stainless steel instruments surrounding the unit seemed to rob him of his normal confidence. 'So I thought I'd wait for you.'

'OK, let's both do it.' She watched the dog's head twitch and saw a fresh spasm of twitching shudder down her whole body. Waiting for it to pass, she stroked the smooth brown and white hair of her neck. 'Ready?' she said to Hoody at last.

Carefully, without putting a strain on the slender catheter tube, they managed to lift the helpless patient and turn her on to her other side. Then Hoody smoothed the fleecy blanket underneath her, while Carly gently massaged her stiff limbs.

31

'We're going to get you better,' she promised as they worked. 'It might not feel like it just yet, but you have to trust us. Dad knows what he's doing. I can tell you he's the best vet around; even if I am his daughter.'

'Huh.' Hoody shrugged. 'You don't think she understands all that, do you?'

'Yes!' Carly muttered back. 'Maybe not word for word. But animals tune into your tone of voice. You know that, don't you?' She went on rubbing, trying to ease the stiffness in the dog's legs.

'But I wouldn't talk to them and think they got all that stuff about trust!'

'Well, they do.' Hoody could like it or lump it, she thought. 'Anyway, I bet you talk to Vinny.'

'Nope.'

'You do. I've heard you.'

'Only "Sit!" and "Stay!" '

'No. You tell him he's a good boy when he fetches a stick or stops at the kerb and waits.'

'That's different,' he argued. 'I wouldn't tell him to trust me. It's not like a stick or a road. You can't see trust, can you?'

Carly sniffed. 'If Vinny was sick, you would.'

'What? Lay the trust stuff on him?' Hoody still scoffed at the idea.

'How much do you bet?'

'Nothing!' He turned away, ready to back off.

'See!' He wouldn't bet. She'd proved her point.

Carly forgot to ask Hoody what he knew about the mysterious leader of the wild dog pack – and now she wouldn't have a chance before she and Steve went to try and bring it in.

It was Saturday afternoon; the surgery was closed and the waiting room at Beech Hill was empty. Liz and Paul were in the operating theatre carrying out the routine operations on their list. Mel was helping with the anaesthetics, while Bupinda was in reception, telephoning owners to give them the latest reports on their sick pets.

'Have you rung round any other vets yet to ask about the missing beagle?' Carly asked, on the way out.

'Not you as well!' Bupinda sighed, cupping her hand over the mouthpiece of the phone. 'Hoody's already been nagging me about that.'

'Sorry.' Carly knew how busy she was.

'I'll do it when I get the time,' the receptionist told her. 'It's on my list!'

So Carly had to be satisfied. She joined Steve by the van in the carpark.

'What do we know about this giant beast?' The inspector leaned on the open car door to discuss tactics. His navy-blue fleece jacket was zipped to the chin to protect him from the cold wind and drizzling rain that quickly collected in a mist of tiny droplets in his thick brown hair. 'Male or female?' he began.

Carly thought hard to recall exactly what Dinky's owner had said. 'Don't know. It's only been around for about a week. It's this big.' She held her hand up to her chest, shivering in the sudden cold. 'It keeps the other dogs in line because of its size. I thought it sounded like a cross between a Great Dane and a mastiff.'

'Hm.' Steve raised his eyebrows. 'Quite a handful.' He glanced inside the van to check that he was carrying a nylon muzzle, a strong rope and padded gloves. 'And what do we know about where they hang out?'

Carly's watch said three o'clock. 'This is the time of day when the pack could still be roaming about on the wasteland at the side of the supermarket.'

'Where they plan to build the big DIY store eventually?' Steve got into the van. 'OK, let's go. It's better to try in daylight. The trick will be to separate this big dog off from the rest and corner him. He's probably hungry, so I've got some dry food to tempt him with. If we're in luck, I'll be able to slip the muzzle on and he'll come quietly.'

She listened as they drove, out of the Rescue Centre and up Beech Hill on to City Road. The windscreen wipers swished and squeaked over the film of dirty moisture thrown up from the road, the traffic-lights flashed green, orange and red as they crawled along the busy dual carriageway.

'Why do you think these dogs hang around so near the main road?' Carly asked. She would have expected them to steer clear of the noise of car engines and their fumes.

'I guess they're scavenging for food.' Steve

signalled right and headed down a sidestreet, then left on to a big expanse of rough, open ground. The site was littered with mounds of broken bricks, lengths of old plastic piping, oil-drums and rotting planks of wood. Puddles of muddy water had formed where car tyres had churned into the ground. Sheets of ripped plastic had caught in a broken barbed-wire fence and flapped in the wind.

Stepping out of the parked van, Carly shivered. The wasteland stretched back towards City Road. In the distance, she thought she spotted Hoody and Vinny passing close by a tall billboard with a torn poster advertising beer. But when she waved to attract their attention, they moved off down the street.

'I don't see any dogs!' Steve announced, turning up his jacket collar and scanning the waste ground. He let his gaze rest on the dull metal roof of Hillman's and the high brick wall between the supermarket and the derelict site. Then his attention wandered to the railway line beyond. 'Are you sure you got this right?' he asked Carly grimly.

'I heard they stuck to the same routine every day,' she insisted. 'And this is where they should be now.'

'Maybe they knew we were coming.' He stamped his cold feet and moved off to look behind a heap of bricks against a half-demolished wall.

Meanwhile, Carly stooped to listen to a scuttling noise she could hear coming from a stack of oil-drums. It sounded like some sort of animal; too big for a mouse or a rat, but with claws that scrabbled and scratched against the rusting metal. *Splash!* The creature, whatever it was, had tried to climb the side of a drum, then seemed to fall back into a puddle in the bottom. Carly located the drum. Gingerly she peered over the top edge into the black space.

'Aagh!' She jumped back and screamed. A pair of bulging lizard-eyes had stared back at her.

Steve came running through the puddles and mud. 'What is it?'

'I don't know. It's enormous!' she gasped. She put her hands to her mouth, then pointed shakily at the drum. 'In there!'

'This one?' The inspector leaned over the side.

'It was like some kind of crocodile, except it can't be!' Carly bit her lip and tiptoed behind Steve. 'Is it still there?'

'Yes, and you're right, it's not a crocodile.' He held out his arm to stop her from getting too close. His own voice was breathless with shock. 'It's a metre-long iguana!'

'What's an iguana doing on a building site?' Mel asked when they took the creature in to Beech Hill. 'Why isn't it in the South American jungle where it belongs?'

Paul Grey viewed the iguana from a safe distance. 'Believe it or not, some people like to keep these as pets.'

The reptile thrashed its scaly, tapering tail and flicked out its long tongue. Its yellow eyes flickered shut, then stared again.

'How did you get it back here?' Bupinda whispered to Carly. Everyone had gathered in the treatment room to see the unusual admission.

'Steve sent me for the biggest pet carrier I could find in the van while he got ready to tip the barrel on to its side,' Carly explained. 'He thinks someone got fed up with feeding it and just dumped it there. Anyway, it was pretty cold and weak by the time we found it.'

'It must have given you the shock of your life,' Mel cut in.

Carly nodded. 'I wish we'd found the giant dog we were looking for rather than this. I just saw its eyes!'

Steve looked across and grinned. 'You did very well. Hardly panicked at all when I tipped the barrel and let it crawl out.'

'By that time I realised how weak it was.' Carly recalled the creature's heavy, sluggish movement on its squat legs. Steve had approached the iguana's head, gripped its jaws together and told her to take the back end. Together they'd lifted it quickly into the carrier, taken it to the van and brought it back to the Rescue Centre.

'It is; *very* weak,' her dad confirmed. 'Not surprising, when you consider its ideal temperature is 35 degrees.' He angled the overhead light to shine directly on the iguana. 'And it probably hasn't been fed properly for months. You see this back leg on the left-hand side? It's broken.'

'From trying to escape from the barrel?' Carly asked. She shuddered as she remembered the sound of the scrabbling claws.

'No. More likely due to lack of calcium in its diet. It should feed on a mixture of flowers, fruit and vegetables, but people don't know what they need when they buy them, so they feed them any old rubbish. Not enough calcium, so the bones grow weak and break under the iguana's own body weight.' He shook his head angrily.

Now Carly felt sorry for the iguana. Ignorant owners had a lot to answer for, she knew. The heavy creature shifted its weight from the broken limb and sank down to rest.

'Shall I get in touch with the reptile house at City Zoo?' Steve suggested.

'Yep. And I'll give it a first shot of calcium,' Paul agreed. 'But don't hold your breath and hope for any miracle cures. This is one sick iguana we have here!'

One sick iguana and no leader of the pack of wild

dogs. Carly sighed and picked up the phone to begin ringing round a list of vets in the city. Bupinda had agreed to let her try and pick up clues about the runaway beagle, knowing that it would keep Carly busy while Steve and Paul were driving the iguana over to the zoo. It was past teatime and already growing dusk.

'. . . No, sorry, I can't help.' A third, and then a fourth attempt brought the same reply. 'We don't have any owners looking for a missing beagle. But keep trying and good luck. I hope you find out who she belongs to.'

Carly put the phone down and crossed another name off the list. It had been an afternoon of dead-ends. She was just going to try a fifth phone call when Hoody came crashing through the door with Vinny.

'You looking for a giant dog?' he cried. He was out of breath, half grinning, half serious.

She dropped the phone. 'Who told you?'

'Mel.' He obviously enjoyed surprising her. 'You were out with Steve at the time. I followed you on foot to the waste ground by the supermarket, but I took one look and knew you

were wasting your time.' Hoody let this sink in,
then threw another question at her. 'So, are you
still looking or not?'

'Yes. Why?' She knew the answer before he
gave it.

'It's in the park. Right this minute. N-O-W,
now. Do you want to come?'

Carly looked over his shoulder through the
glass doors. 'It's getting dark.' *Feeble*! she told
herself. *What a wimpy thing to say!*

'So?' His eyes were wide and glittering, his
chest heaved in and out.

'OK!' She left the list of vets' names on the desk
and dashed for the door. 'Come on, what are we
waiting for?'

Together they ran out on to the pavement and
down the hill towards the park. They took a side
alleyway between the gardens of two big, old
houses, through a tunnel of overhanging bushes
which opened out on to a steep grassy slope, with
a long, narrow lake at the bottom and more grass
and trees beyond that. The rain came down in a
fine drizzle which was gusted into their faces by
a cold wind.

'Where?' Carly gasped. The park seemed dark and quiet. Overhead, the beech trees shook showers of dead leaves to the ground.

'Across the lake.' Hoody led the way, with Vinny trotting quietly at his heels. 'You're never gonna believe this, Carly,' he whispered. 'This has gotta be the most brilliant dog you've ever seen!'

4

A stream ran through Beech Hill Park into the lake. The banks of the stream were lined with laurel bushes, and this was where the pack of wild dogs had gathered.

Carly stopped short as she saw them milling about in the half-light, heads up, ears pricked, their hot breath sending clouds of steam into the cold air. There were dogs with shaggy coats, their faces almost hidden behind a mass of tangled fur and others, lean and whippet-like, with short, dark coats and narrow, hungry faces. Most were crossbreeds; a dozen or so dogs that nobody wanted, pets that had been cruelly treated and turned out of their homes.

'Where's the leader?' she whispered.

Hoody held on to Vinny, whose hackles had risen. Though he was outnumbered twelve to one, the squat little mongrel was all set to hold his ground against the pack. 'It won't be far away,' he promised.

Leaves in a bush on the opposite bank rustled, heavy steps snapped twigs underfoot. A huge, dark shape emerged from the shadows.

Vinny growled and crouched low. 'Here it comes!' Hoody whispered.

Carly held her breath. The dog was a giant: tall as a Great Dane, with the same sleek coat, but much heavier. His square head was massive, with large, drooping ears, a broad, dark muzzle and jowls that fell softly over a sad-looking mouth. But, in spite of his terrifying size, it was the eyes that held her.

The dog had come out of the bushes at the sound of their approach and fixed them with its gaze. His eyes caught the last light and burnt a deep amber; steady, brave eyes on the lookout for danger. Round, sad eyes that seemed to ask them if they were friend or foe.

As their leader stood at the top of the bank, towering over them, the rest of the dogs in the pack fell quiet and still. Vinny stopped growling and backed off behind Hoody.

'Amazing!' Carly breathed. She felt held under a magic spell, fixed by the burning eyes.

Still wary, the dog came down the far bank and stepped through the running water, surefooted between the boulders. His giant stride brought him in amongst the pack, close to where Carly and Hoody stood.

The other dogs waited – all except one half-starved creature, a grey German shepherd-cross with the air of a hungry wolf. It broke away and came looking for Vinny, hackles raised, teeth bared.

Wisely, Hoody's dog lowered his head and crouched low. He didn't want a fight. But the wild dog snarled a challenge. The hair round his sharp face was matted with dirt and burrs, his fangs were long and yellow as he snapped his jaws within centimetres of Vinny's face.

'Stay back!' Hoody warned his dog not to retaliate.

Vinny obeyed, watching the wild dog's every move. In the background, the pack jostled uneasily.

Again the grey dog snapped and snarled. He moved in, ready to pounce.

But the huge, fawn leader of the pack loped silently forward. Like a pale shadow, he came between the angry pack member and Vinny, warning the aggressor off. The grey dog laid back his pointed ears and snarled. Then he gave way.

Carly sighed with relief that the huge dog had prevented the fight. Vinny was tough, but he stood no chance against a whole pack. As the fierce grey dog rejoined the rest, she caught sight of Hoody's tense, pale face. 'You were right: that is one brilliant dog!' she breathed.

And now he was loping round the outside of the pack, head up, sniffing the air. The dogs were no longer on edge, but milling quietly again, and Carly could see that most were in poor condition, covered in sores like the beagle at the Rescue

Centre, some limping, all hungry. She pictured meals scavenged from bins and rubbish-tips, a life of being hounded and chased out into the cold and damp. Winter was coming. What would the dogs do then?

'We have to help them,' she decided afresh.

'Yeah.' Hoody frowned. 'Like, they're really gonna be grateful if we lock them in a kennel.'

'They'll probably die if we don't.' In the frost and snow, the freezing winter fogs and short, dark days.

'So, how?' He spoke in snatched sentences, looking angry, not at the dogs but at the whole world.

'We have to capture the leader first.' Without him, the others would be easier to split up and take in.

'Right.' Hoody was sarcastic. 'Like, I've got Vinny's lead in my pocket. Shall I just go up and slip it on? "We'd like a word with you down at the station if you don't mind, sir!" '

Carly grunted. 'Steve thinks we'll be able to tempt him with food.' She watched the strong dog retrace his steps down the bank and through the cold stream, taking the others with him this time. One by one, the dogs disappeared into the laurel bushes.

'Sorry!' Hoody turned his pockets inside out to show they were empty. 'I didn't bring any with me!'

'Not now. Next time.' They were nowhere near capturing him on this first close encounter. She glimpsed his massive form between the dark leaves and low branches, saw him emerge from the bushes, lope a hundred metres towards the houses on Ash Grove, then stand silhouetted at the top of the slope. Eagerly the other dogs followed.

'If there is a next time.'

'What do you mean?'

'I mean, if he lets you get near him a second time,' Hoody insisted. 'I reckon he won't.'

'Why not?'

'Not if he's got any sense, he won't. It's like a wild animal, isn't it? They don't let you get too close. And dogs are clever. He probably knows what you're planning.'

'How?' Carly demanded. In the distance, at the

border of the park, the pack gathered around the leader.

Hoody shrugged. 'You're the one who thinks dogs can understand what you're saying,' he retorted. 'So I reckon you can take it one step further and say they can read your mind as well.'

He made it sound like magic, out there in the gloomy, windswept park. Like the dog was a magician using a sixth sense to read her thoughts. As the giant stray threw back his head, opened his mouth and howled, she thought of the perfect name.

'Merlin!' she whispered.

The howl pierced the black sky and echoed round the park. In the road beyond, headlights glared. When the car had passed and left the grassy slope in darkness once more, Merlin and his pack had vanished into thin air.

'Even Steve needs a day off occasionally,' Paul Grey told Carly next day.

It was a frosty Sunday morning, and the Rescue Centre was quiet. Only Carly and her dad were there to feed and clean the animals, while the rest of the staff took a well-deserved break.

Carly had got up and come down from the flat as soon as she was washed and dressed, to find her dad already at work. Her first question had been about Merlin.

'You know Hoody showed me the leader of the dogs that are running wild in the park?' She'd rushed home to tell her dad, describing the magnificent dog in every detail. 'Will Steve help us to catch him?'

'When?' Paul had glanced up from weighing a hedgehog on some scales. The tiny creature had tucked its head and legs out of sight and curled into a ball, spikes bristling.

'Today.' Now that she'd seen Merlin at close quarters, she was keen to act.

That was when her dad had said that Steve wouldn't be in. He saw Carly's face fall. 'How come it's so urgent?' he asked, carefully picking the hedgehog off the scales with a padded glove and returning it to its snug nesting-box on the table.

She swallowed her disappointment. 'It isn't dead urgent,' she confessed. 'Only, the days are getting colder, and I really want to help, but there's no way that Hoody and I could bring this dog in by ourselves.'

'Quite right.' Paul smiled at her for being sensible for once. 'Write down "520 grammes" on the hedgehog's weight chart for me, please.'

'She's put on another eight grammes.' Carly filled in the chart. 'That's thirty-two grammes since she was brought in.'

The hedgehog had been found in a garden on King Edward's Road by kids who had been building a bonfire for November the fifth. They'd dug it out of a hedge bottom and, listening to its noisy, snuffly breathing, realised something was wrong and brought it straight to Beech Hill. Liz had diagnosed a chest infection and begun a treatment of antibiotics, vitamins and good food. The hedgehog had recovered from the infection and quickly put on weight. Soon she would be ready to return to the wild.

'That's one success story to set against our recent failure.' Paul moved on from the hedgehog to the budgie in its cage. He opened the door and reached in to let it hop on to his finger.

'Isn't he any better?' Carly asked anxiously. She hadn't thought scaly beak was a serious condition.

'It's not the budgie I mean. It's the iguana.'

'Why? What's happened?' She handed him a cotton bud for him to dip into the small jar of liquid.

'I had a phone call from the zoo last night. The reptile section did everything they could – put him in a special unit with ultraviolet light and a humidifier – but I'm afraid he didn't make it. He died just a few hours after we left him there.'

Carly frowned and shook her head. 'This is a bad weekend.'

'I know. I'm sorry.' Her dad finished with the cotton bud, stroked the bird's chest with his forefinger and put him back in the cage. 'I tell you what: even though Steve isn't in today, there's no reason why you and I shouldn't take a look at this amazing dog you're telling me about, is there?'

She gasped and squeezed between him and the hedgehog's nesting-box, staring eagerly at him. 'Really?'

He nodded. 'Later. When I've finished the ward rounds and you've cleaned out the kennels, and we've done the hundred and one things we have to do. We could combine it with taking our little friend here down to the park and finding a nice quiet corner for her to make her winter's nest.' He tapped the hedgehog's box. 'I'm quite happy with her now that she's put on enough weight to see her through the winter.'

'That would be great,' Carly agreed.

'Late this afternoon, then. Tell Hoody. No doubt he'll want to be in on this.'

'OK.' Her spirits were rising after the bad news from the zoo. She gave her dad a bright grin as she rushed off to call on her friend. 'And this time, I'll tell him he'd better leave Vinny at home!'

Hoody arrived at five, pretending to be casual and couldn't-care-less as he strolled into Beech Hill and came looking for Carly in intensive care.

She was crouched by the see-through unit, checking the level of fluid in the beagle's drip, when she saw Hoody's figure, distorted by the moulded plastic. She stood up straight, making him jump. 'You're early!'

'So?'

'Dad's not quite ready. Do you want to help me turn the patient?'

He grunted, then nodded. 'How is she?'

'Holding her own. Still weak.' Carly had popped in many times during the day to nurse the dog through the long hours of pain and confusion.

'She's still having these fit things.' There was a scared look in Hoody's eyes as he watched the muscles twitch and shudder.

'Yes, but not so often.' She guessed the reason why he was hanging back. 'Don't worry, you can touch her. It doesn't hurt her.'

Hoody sniffed. He knocked the blue identification card out of its clip as he leaned in awkwardly to help Carly lift. Afterwards, when the beagle had been turned on to her other side and lay looking helplessly at them, he stooped to pick it up. 'What's this code, STR22, still doing here?' he demanded. 'Why hasn't she got a name?'

Carly felt her face flush. 'I suppose it's because I didn't want to get too attached,' she confessed. Giving a dog a name made her grow fond of it. 'In case she doesn't make it.'

'What sort of reason's that?' he scoffed. 'You gave Merlin a name, didn't you?'

'So?' She played him at his own game, shooting a sullen question back at him.

'So, you can't just call this one letters and numbers!' He meant it. He was genuinely angry.

'So, *you* choose one!' Carly glared back at him, then turned to go and see if her dad was ready to take the hedgehog to the park. She flung a pen at him. 'When you've decided, write it down on the card!'

Five minutes later, after Carly had found Paul, then nipped upstairs for their jackets, she slipped back into intensive care to see the beagle. The dog was sleeping peacefully for once under the bright, warm lights of the unit. The blue card was back in place. 'STR22' was scribbled out, replaced by a name written in Hoody's spidery hand.

Carly made it out, then gazed for a few seconds

at the sleeping dog. 'Hazel,' she murmured, and smiled. 'Sleep well.'

The little hedgehog trundled out of the nesting-box into the chilly evening air. Her pointed snout sniffed the damp, rotting leaves and earth smells of the park. Her beady, short-sighted eyes peered through the gloom.

Carly glanced anxiously at her dad. It seemed like a big, dangerous world for the tiny creature to survive in.

'Don't worry, she'll soon get her bearings,' Paul Grey promised.

And, true enough, the hedgehog seemed to like what she found: the piles of dead leaves hid insects and beetles which she could root out with her long snout, the twigs in the hedge bottom would make a good beginning for her new nest. Soon she was scuttling through the grass, digging for worms with her sharp claws, sniffing and snuffling to her heart's content.

'Mission accomplished,' Paul said softly to Carly and Hoody. The hedgehog had vanished at last in amongst the tangled roots of a hawthorn hedge. 'Now for this mysterious dog I keep hearing about!'

Carly braced herself. It was the right time, the right place to see the magnificent creature. Yet half of her drew back from the plan. She scanned the park and zipped her jacket to the chin. 'Are you sure we should catch him?'

'I thought that was the general idea.' Paul had brought food, rope and muzzle, prepared to trap the stray and take him back with them.

'He'll never fall for it – you wait,' Hoody muttered.

'We'll see.' Carly's dad told them that a starving animal would take great risks to get food. 'Just show me where the pack hangs out, and I'll leave some out as a bait.'

So they took him to the stream, where he left handfuls of biscuits on flat stones at the water's edge. Then they hid in the laurel bushes and settled down to wait. Daylight faded from the clear sky and it grew freezing cold.

A low howl warned them that the pack was near. Ducks on the lake rose and flapped clumsily overhead. A man pushing his bike hurried along the path . . . and then the dogs appeared.

Merlin led them down the slope from the gates on Beech Hill. He loped easily, his wide stride eating up the ground, while the smaller dogs scuttled along after him.

'Wow!' Paul Grey was impressed. He crouched low, the rope coiled in one hand, the muzzle stuffed into his jacket pocket. 'No wonder people don't want to mess with him!'

The pack had reached the lake and stopped. Merlin waited for the stragglers: a small white terrier type and a shivering brown crossbreed who came limping along last of all. By now, some of the dogs must have smelled the food that Paul had used as a bait, for they broke off from the main group and ranged swiftly up the slope along the banks of the stream.

Carly held her breath, her eyes fixed on Merlin. The big dog waited for the last in the pack, then herded them after the rest. By the time they reached the bait, the fitter, faster dogs had wolfed it down. The savage grey German shepherd-cross fought off the tired late-comers as they sniffed for overlooked crumbs. He snarled and snapped, then splashed down into the stream to drink.

Slowly, cautiously, Merlin followed. He seemed to be listening, glancing at the bushes where Carly, Hoody and Paul hid.

'Ssh!' Paul held up a warning finger. The huge dog was less than ten metres away. They could see his gleaming amber eyes, hear his tongue lapping water from the stream. Carly's dad gripped the rope in both hands and crept clear of the bush.

Merlin saw him and reared up. The huge dog jerked away and stumbled against a boulder, as the grey stray grew alarmed and sped up the opposite bank, setting off a stampede that took the fit members of the pack away from the stream, across the flat expanse towards Ash Grove. Only the two weak stragglers stayed to see what happened to their leader.

Carly saw Merlin miss his footing and fall. She gasped and put her hand to her mouth as her father slid down the slope towards him. Hoody followed, scrambling down the bank, losing his balance and splashing into the shallow water.

Paul Grey reached the stream. He could almost stretch out and touch Merlin, who struggled to his feet. The eyes of the dog bored into the man, questioning him, growing suspicious of the rope in his hands. Ropes meant traps, betrayal, loss of freedom. No, he wouldn't trust the vet!

Suddenly he turned and surged away, his strong, smooth body bounding clear of the stream, his huge feet pounding the ground.

'Quick!' Carly knew they'd lost their chance with Merlin. But the two injured dogs were slower. They whined and struggled to follow as the pack left them behind. 'We can still capture these two!'

She ran down the bank and leaped across the stream, then scrambled up the other side, using her hands to steady herself. Then she was up and chasing the small white dog. She glimpsed Hoody close behind her, set on catching the brown mongrel.

The dogs yelped and cried out. They were weak and confused, too slow to escape. Carly's dog stumbled and fell. As he rolled, she took off her jacket and threw it over him, wrapping him in it and clutching the whole thing to her.

Hoody's dog was even slower. Her limp made her whine with every step. He only had to run alongside her and scoop her up. She didn't even protest as she gave up the struggle and sank crying into his arms.

5

'You know what amazes me?' Paul Grey showed Steve Winter the two new arrivals when he came to work early next morning. Carly's dad held the small white dog under his arm. The bigger, brown stray sat quietly at his feet, her front leg bandaged.

'How people can be so cruel as to dump their dogs and leave them to starve!' Carly took a guess at what her dad would say next. She'd slipped into the kennels before she left for school and found him and the inspector discussing the strays.

Paul shook his head. 'No. I've got used to that, worse luck. No, what really stuns me is the way the dogs always forgive us humans after all we've done to them.'

Carly looked at the small white terrier cross-breed. He snuggled up to her dad and licked his hand, proof that his loving nature had survived the cruel treatment of his ex-owner.

'Who knows what drove him to join the feral pack in the first place?' Paul went on. 'Maybe someone beat him or starved him, left him alone for days on end, or kicked him out for good.'

Carly frowned. She put her schoolbag on the floor and crouched beside the brown dog to stroke her too.

'Yet show this same dog a drop of kindness, and he forgets the past. He's as loving and trusting as if it had never happened.' Her dad sounded sad and wistful as he gave the white dog a final pat and put him into his kennel.

The dog whined and tried to creep out again. He wagged his stumpy tail and gazed at Carly's dad with sorrowful eyes. *Please let me out!*

'Oh, OK, just for a few more minutes.' Paul weakened and opened the door.

Steve smiled. 'Someone give that dog an Oscar for best actor!'

'That's it!' Carly grinned too as the dog wheedled his way out of the kennel. 'Let's call him Oscar!' For some reason it suited him. 'And you can be Rosie,' she told the lame dog gently. 'But don't ask me why.'

'Oscar and Rosie,' Paul agreed.

The two dogs wagged their tails at him and followed in his footsteps everywhere he went, from one kennel to the next on his morning rounds.

Glancing at the wall-clock in the corridor, Carly saw that unless she hurried she would be late for school.

'What next?' she asked, before she dashed off.

'For Oscar and Rosie?' Her dad persuaded the dogs into their kennels at last. As he hardened his heart to lock the doors, he gave Carly a quick rundown on what would happen to them now. 'The same as for the beagle. We ask Bupinda to have a go at tracing an owner. But that's a long shot, so the likely outcome is that we'll be looking to rehome them if we can.'

And if we can't? The question sprang to Carly's mind, but she didn't come out with it. Living here at Beech Hill, she knew the answer only too well: *If we can't find a new home for Hazel, and for Oscar and Rosie, eventually we have no alternative but to put them to sleep.*

'Rosie looks a bit like Vinny,' Carly decided. She compared the brindle stripes on the stray dog's back with Vinny's short, wiry coat.

They were walking the dogs in the park after school, giving Rosie some exercise now that her leg was beginning to heal. It was three days since they'd brought her in and treated her with antibiotics for the infected cut that had caused the limp. She'd been cleaned, fed the right diet, vaccinated and wormed. Soon she would be perfectly fit and well. But still homeless.

'She doesn't look anything like him,' Hoody retorted. To him, Vinny's sturdy body, white chest and broad, friendly face made him unique.

Carly crossed the paved play area and

slumped on to a damp swing. 'You know we haven't been able to trace any owners yet.' Bupinda had tried. She'd circulated details about the three stray dogs around all the city vets. Each time the answer had come back: 'No, sorry. I'm afraid we can't help.'

'So, tell me something new.' Hoody picked up a stick and threw it for the two dogs. It flew in a shallow arc across the level ground marked out as a football pitch. Vinny raced through the drizzle, falling over himself and rolling in the mud in his eagerness to retrieve it.

Poor Rosie hobbled along after.

'Something new is that Hazel drank water for the first time today.' Five days after the dog had been brought in, Carly's dad had greeted her arrival home from school with the news that the beagle had taken liquid by mouth.

'Is that good?' Hoody asked.

She nodded and began to swing, kicking herself off then using her legs to gain height. 'Dad says it means the muscles in her face are beginning to unlock. She can actually swallow now. And she can stand if someone helps her up.'

'But she can't walk?' He took the stick from Vinny and threw it again.

'Not yet. What do you want: miracles?' Why couldn't Hoody just be pleased with Hazel's progress so far?

He shrugged, then grinned up at her as she flew past on the swing. 'A miracle might be OK every now and then.'

'I'll mention it to Dad: "One miracle cure, please!" ' Carly laughed. She launched herself from the moving swing and landed nimbly. 'Come and see for yourself how Hazel is,' she suggested.

They put Vinny and Rosie on the lead and were on their way up the path towards the main gates when they saw Merlin for the first time that week.

Since Sunday, the dog had steered well clear of Steve Winter and his ropes and muzzles. Steve had been out twice during daylight hours to try and bring the leader of the pack back to Beech Hill, but each time Merlin had slipped away. The inspector said his name should be Houdini – not Merlin – after the famous escapologist.

'The dog that can't be captured,' Paul Grey had said after Steve's second failure.

'The invisible dog!' Carly had added. She and Hoody had been out looking for him each day after school, but Merlin had kept well out of their way.

Now, though, the massive dog decided to put in an appearance.

At first they thought he was alone. He appeared between the stone gateposts, alert as always, and stood for a few moments surveying the park. Seeing Carly and Hoody with their two dogs, he gave a warning bark to the pack behind him. The bark came from deep in his great chest, and echoed across the green slopes. It made the hairs at the back of Carly's neck stand on end.

'He remembers us from last Sunday!' Hoody hissed. 'He thinks we're gonna take more of the pack and put them behind bars!'

Ten or eleven stray dogs came up from behind and gathered round their leader at the gates. In the background, the streetlights on Beech Hill flickered pink, then glared orange over the steady stream of rush-hour traffic.

'Look at Rosie!' Carly felt her strain at the lead, eager to rejoin her group. At the same time, Merlin seemed to recognise the brown dog. He cocked his head to one side, took a few steps down the slope, stopped and stared. The other dogs milled uneasily at the gates.

Again Merlin opened his huge mouth and barked. Vinny stayed quietly by Hoody's side as Rosie barked back with a high, excited yap.

Then, out of nowhere, the tense waiting game blew apart. Three boys on mountain bikes came speeding through the park gates. They reared them up like bucking horses, swerved them and raced through the pack of dogs, bodies crouched low over the handlebars, daring each other to take the lead.

'Idiots,' Hoody muttered.

The screech of brakes and the skidding of tyres alarmed the dogs in the gathering dusk. They scattered across the slope, leaving Merlin to stand alone.

Determined to show off in front of his audience of Hoody and Carly, one boy rode straight at the giant dog. He stood up from the saddle, yelling at the top of his voice.

Merlin froze, head down, front legs splayed wide, ready for the impact.

'Stop!' Carly cried.

At the last second, the boy braked and swerved. He pedalled off laughing, looking over his shoulder to check that the dog wasn't following him.

'Idiots!' Hoody said again. 'Merlin could've bitten a chunk out of his leg if he'd wanted to!' Despite his size, they were beginning to understand that the dog didn't retaliate even when provoked.

Carly watched him now, taking stock of the scattered pack and the jeering boys, of her and Hoody quietly watching from the sidelines with Vinny and Rosie. 'He obviously didn't want to,' she murmured, fascinated by Merlin, his size, his gentleness. 'It's as if he knows he could do a lot of damage with those teeth, so he holds back.'

Hoody agreed. 'No way is he wild, like they say. Far from it. He's better trained than those idiots on the bikes for a start.'

'But try telling other people that.' Carly watched Merlin watching them. Back to the old, cautious waiting game. She held tight to Rosie, who still wanted to join her old friend. 'They take one look at him and say he's dangerous.'

'They don't know what they're talking about!' Hoody grew impatient. 'They haven't even bothered to find out!'

'Maybe it's because he sounds wild.'

As if on cue, Merlin tilted his head back, opened his mouth and howled. The other members of the pack came running from all corners of the park to his call.

Hoody dropped his head towards his chest to think. 'We're saying Merlin is the dog that can't be captured, but we're also saying he isn't wild, right?'

Carly nodded.

'So that means someone, somewhere, did own him?'

'Like Rosie, Oscar and Hazel once had owners; yeah.' It figured.

Hoody frowned. 'So, how can you lose a dog that big?'

'You mean, unless it's on purpose?' She began to follow his line of thought.

'Or, unless something happens to you and it means you can't look after him any more. Like you die, say!' Hoody's eyes gathered intensity as he looked up and stared at Carly.

'Or have an accident, or move house and your dog gets lost somehow.' She painted a less final picture of what could have happened to Merlin's owner.

'Are you thinking what I'm thinking?' Hoody swung round to see what the dogs were up to now. He saw them gathered into a tight pack, trotting down to the lake, following their usual evening route.

'That maybe we shouldn't be concentrating on trying to catch Merlin?' Carly said slowly. 'That, if we really want to do what's best for him, we should look for his owner instead?'

Hoody nodded. His gaze followed the dogs through the gloomy evening. Merlin led them along the lakeside, across the stream into the dark bushes. One by one they disappeared from view.

73

'He comes here every night – same time, same time, same place,' Hoody said, slowly turning things over in his mind. 'He's the one who decides on the route; not any of the others.'

'Yes,' Carly agreed.

'So, why? Why here? Where is he heading?'

'Ash Grove.' To terrify the families who only glimpsed his enormous, shadowy shape in the bushes at the end of their gardens.

'But where exactly?' Hoody insisted. Suddenly it was a matter of life and death.

One particular street? One house or flat? Carly had no idea. But she spotted the pack of dogs run clear of the bushes by the stream, loping after Merlin towards the streetlights of Ash Grove.

She felt Rosie tug at the lead. That was it! Rosie would know from her time with the pack where the dogs were heading.

And, if Hoody was guessing right, catching up with the dogs after they left the park might give them a clue that would lead them to Merlin's owner.

But Carly still hadn't answered Hoody's question. 'Where exactly is Merlin heading?'

'Let's find out!' she said suddenly, giving Rosie her head and letting the eager stray lead them across the darkening park.

6

'Are you sure this is the right way?' Hoody pulled up on a corner to catch his breath. For more than half an hour Rosie had led them down a maze of back streets without giving them a single sighting of Merlin and the rest of the pack.

Carly nodded. They'd come all the way down Ash Grove, past the tall Victorian houses with the big gardens overlooking the park. Then they'd cut off through rows of terraced cottages built close together and facing straight on to the street. They all looked the same: row after row of brick houses with grey slate roofs and wet stone pavements shining orange under the streetlamps. 'Trust Rosie,' she told Hoody. 'She knows where she's going.'

'Let's hope so.' He looked and listened down the next street. ' "Prospect Road",' he read on the sign fixed to the front wall of the corner house.

Carly set off again with Rosie. 'This was your fault. You gave me the idea!' she reminded him. She could see the lights from a small shop on the next corner. Perhaps they should ask there about the route the dogs had taken.

'Yes, but I never knew they came this far. I thought they stuck to the streets around Beech Hill.' Hoody didn't feel so confident off his own patch, where he knew everyone and everything that went on. This area of narrow streets and dark alleyways that led into closed backyards, seemed like a strange, unfriendly maze.

'Did a pack of stray dogs come this way?' Carly ignored Hoody's doubts and asked a dark-haired girl who had just come out of the corner shop carrying a newspaper and a can of Coke.

The girl eyed Rosie and Vinny suspiciously, and drew back up the step.

'Strays?' The shopkeeper overheard and came out from behind his counter. He was a small, dark-skinned man with neat, black hair, a black moustache and a soft, musical voice. 'You mean the ones with the giant dog leading them? They're always hanging about round here; a real menace. I don't know why somebody doesn't do something about them.' He launched into a long, slow complaint.

'Yes, but did you just see them?' Carly interrupted. She let Rosie sniff around the doorstep and the litter bin, and felt her pull at the lead again.

'Of course.' The shopkeeper nodded. 'Always at this time, running wild along the street. If you ask me, it's getting much worse. The pack is growing bigger. And there's the dog we're all scared of: the huge one with the terrible bark . . .'

'Thanks,' Hoody interrupted. He thought of a question that might mean he and Carly could stop trailing the dogs from street to street and reach their next stopping-off place ahead of them. 'Do you know where they end up after they've run past here?'

The shopkeeper thought for a few seconds. 'I don't know that they end up anywhere. They're always on the move.' He seemed sorry that he couldn't help.

'No.' The girl with the newspaper spoke for the first time through a mouthful of chewing-gum. 'They do stop. They have to sleep, don't they?'

This was true. Carly jumped in to ask the vital question. 'Do you know where?'

The girl sniffed and shrugged. 'In some old place by the canal. I'm not sure exactly.'

What did she mean, an 'old place'? 'A warehouse? A factory?' Hoody prompted.

'No. It's by the flyover they've just built. There's a big old house nearby. It's split up into flats, but everyone had to move out when they built the road. From what I hear, it's empty during the day, but at night it's overrun with these stray dogs.'

'Thanks!' The canal, the new flyover, a big

house – Carly was sure they could find it. She turned to Hoody.

'Come on, what are we waiting for?' he said, setting off with Vinny for the newly built road over the canal.

The gleaming flyover stood on tall, fat concrete legs. Beneath it, the old brick warehouses were dwarfed and grimy. Wind blew through the gaping, broken windows, roof tiles had slipped and crashed on to the wharves below.

Carly stood by a concrete pillar, huddled inside her warm fleece jacket. She hated the place the moment she saw it. The grey canal water looked greasy, the vast, empty buildings somehow sad and eerie.

'Where's this house?' Hoody demanded, letting Vinny off the lead to sniff around the deserted wharves.

'I don't know.' There didn't seem to be a house; only the depressing, derelict warehouses. Carly realised, as she set Rosie loose too, that they were relying on an unknown girl's word. Maybe she'd made a mistake, or sent them off on the wrong track as her idea of a joke.

'And where's the pack of dogs?' Hoody strode under the flyover after Vinny and Rosie, vanishing into thick shadow.

There was no sign of life in the overgrown yards; only the rattle of an empty can as it rolled along the stone cobbles in the wind. 'Not here yet?' she suggested quietly, knowing that Hoody was already out of earshot.

'Carly!' His voice yelled for her to come quick.

She ran into the shadow of the flyover, heard the traffic rumble overhead, came out at the far side to find Hoody holding on to Vinny and Rosie's collars. He was staring at a house – *the* house where the stray dogs gathered.

It was squeezed between another warehouse and a two-storey factory built of glass and steel. Behind it, a tall office-block rose into a dark-grey sky. The house had been there first, but now the newer, bigger buildings seemed to be squashing it forwards and into the canal, so that its shadow crept to the very brink of the stagnant water.

It had once been a solid, respectable house, Carly could tell. There was a stone porch with pillars outside the front door, big windows to either side. But now the brick walls were black from centuries of soot, the windows boarded up against vandals. Iron railings that ran along the front and up the sides of the house were rusting and twisted, the garden a rubbish tip for old sofas, car tyres and rolls of rotting carpet.

Hoody crouched at the water's edge beside Vinny and Rosie, holding on to their collars. 'The dogs are here!' he whispered.

'How do you know?' To her, the miserable house looked deserted.

'I heard a noise from inside.'

'You're sure it was them?' Carly found she was shivering as she stared through the gloom at the blank, boarded windows.

'Yes. Look at Rosie.'

She saw the stray straining to free herself from Hoody's grasp. She wriggled and pulled, then let out a loud, sharp bark.

Carly jumped, then steadied herself against the iron railings. An unseen dog gave a deep, roaring reply.

'Merlin!' Hoody said quietly.

Round the back of the house, other dogs yapped and barked. Soon, the giant dog himself padded into view.

'Duck!' Carly dived down behind a low wall. She didn't want to scare Merlin off after all this effort.

'Too late. He's seen us.' Hoody didn't hide. 'It's OK, he doesn't mind.'

Grasping the cold iron poles, she peered over the wall. Merlin seemed to have realised without surprise that he was being followed. He wagged his long, thin tail at Rosie and came a few more steps forward.

Rosie whined and struggled.

'Hold on to her!' Carly urged.

'That's what I'm trying to do.' Hoody spoke through gritted teeth. 'Listen, this is useless. We're never gonna get in there and look for clues about Merlin with the dogs running loose!'

'Clues,' Carly echoed. Some small piece of evidence that might show them why Merlin led the pack here each night. Was there a special reason? Or was it simply because the empty house gave them shelter from the wind and rain?

Maybe it was sheer chance that had first brought them to the house by the canal.

As Merlin stood in the wrecked garden, silently watching them, and the other dogs kept well out of sight, Hoody was forced to admit defeat. 'Yeah,' he said in a flat voice. 'This is a dead-end, isn't it?'

'Maybe.' She was edgy, disappointed. 'Maybe not.' In any case, Hoody was right about one thing: they wouldn't get the chance to find out while the dogs were there. 'We could come back in the morning when they're not around.'

Relieved, Hoody nodded and turned with Vinny and Rosie, heading back under the flyover. Carly stayed a few seconds longer. Enough time for Merlin to catch her eye again. He gazed at her with his sad, intelligent face, looking for all the world as if he longed for her to understand the whole mystery of why he was there.

The eerie feeling was so strong that Carly opened her mouth and spoke to the powerful, silent dog.

'What are you up to?' she whispered. 'Are we on the right track? Or are we wasting our time?'

*

'Listen to me very carefully!' Paul Grey sat Carly and Hoody down in the waiting area at Beech Hill.

He'd been standing by the door when they got back from the canal, seeing out the last patient after evening surgery. Carly had been able to tell with one quick glance that he was angry.

Quickly she'd taken Rosie back to her kennel and rejoined her dad, Vinny and Hoody in the empty waiting room. Now she sat under the colourful photographs of the dogs and cats that Beech Hill had recently rescued and rehomed. From the expression on her dad's face, she expected the worst.

'Hoody tells me you've been trying to track down the feral dogs again,' Paul said sternly. He stood over them, a stethoscope dangling from the pocket of his white coat, his tie loose and shirt unbuttoned at the collar.

Carly nodded.

'You went as far as Newton Flyover?' Without waiting for an answer, he listed on his fingers the things they'd done wrong. 'First, you did this without telling me. As far as I knew, you were walking the dogs in the park. When you didn't come straight back, I was worried. Yet that consideration never seems to have crossed your minds.

'Second, it was getting dark. And yes, I know you had two dogs with you, but even so there was no guarantee you'd be safe. This was an area you don't know at all, either of you. You could've got lost, had an accident, been attacked, fallen into the canal . . . !' He glared at them both, only pausing for breath before he went on.

'Third, these dogs you were tracking could very well be dangerous!'

Carly swallowed hard. She wanted to argue back, to say that Merlin wasn't a danger to anyone, that they were sure they could find out more about him by following in his tracks and working out the reason behind his movements. But her father was hardly ever angry, and when he was it was best to keep quiet.

'I know what you're thinking!' Paul's eyes bored into her. 'You don't believe the dogs would attack you. They're all like Rosie and Oscar:

cuddly, lovable creatures who wouldn't harm a fly!'

'We're not saying that.' Hoody spoke up at last.

'No?'

'No. We realise there's one dog that's pretty vicious.' Hoody's face was red, he stared at the floor and shuffled his feet under the bench.

Carly knew which one he meant: the grey German shepherd-cross that had picked a fight with Vinny.

'So, one is enough.' Paul pointed out that they would have to learn the hard way if the dog got the chance to sink its teeth into their legs. He made them listen to the rules he wanted them to follow. 'What I'm telling you is that you stay well away from this pack from now on. You don't go near that flyover when they're around; not for any reason. Got it?'

This was hard. It was like asking them to give up on Merlin. Carly hesitated and hung her head.

'Leave it to Steve,' her dad insisted. 'It's his job to bring these strays in for rehoming. Let him do it his way, in his own time, OK?'

Hoody jerked to his feet, muttering under his

breath. Carly caught the words, 'No way'.

'What was that?' Paul turned sharply.

'I said that no way does bringing Merlin into Beech Hill give him a fair chance.' Hoody jutted out his chin and spoke defiantly.

Carly's dad ran a weary hand across his face. He didn't have the strength to argue. 'Spare us the melodrama, please, Hoody.'

The boy was on his way out with Vinny. He knocked clumsily against a rack of pamphlets, and didn't stop to pick up the ones that slipped and fluttered to the floor.

Carly ran after him. 'Stop a second. What do you mean?'

He walked on, out through the doors, across the carpark. But before he disappeared on to Beech Hill, he flung an explanation back at her.

'Think about it. Who wants Hazel? Nobody. Who wants Oscar or Rosie? Nobody.'

'So?'

'So what chance has Merlin got if they bring him in? *Zilcho*. Big fat no chance. So don't talk to me about rehoming, 'cos it's not gonna happen!'

Behind her, Carly sensed her tired father

listening and sighing. She tried to shut the door on Hoody's angry final words.

'You want the truth?' he yelled at Carly, walking backwards, spreading his arms in a gesture of frustration. 'Face it, Carly, in the end they'll have to put him down. They're signing Merlin's death certificate if they bring him in here!'

7

For the rest of that week, Carly felt pulled in two.

Yes, Hoody was probably right. Merlin *might* be doomed to die. Her friend's sullen silence at school during the days following the argument with her dad reminded her of the threat hanging over the dog's head. The thought made the sign above the door, 'Beech Hill Rescue Centre', seem hollow every time she came home and passed under it.

But on the other hand, Carly trusted her father and wanted to believe that bringing Merlin in to the Centre would be for the best. They would feed him and look after him, let him know that not all humans were cruel and hostile. Meanwhile, the whole neigbourhood would relax. No more terrifying encounters at dusk, no more fear of the giant dog running wild. Weeks would pass. Without their leader the stray dogs would change their pattern. They might split up and drift across the city to other estates and tower blocks, become somebody else's problem . . .

Carly sighed. It was Saturday morning, and still Merlin refused to be captured. Steve had tried again on Thursday night. He'd brought in another member of the pack, but got nowhere near Merlin. He said he'd come close to being bitten by the fierce German shepherd type and beaten a hasty retreat. Meanwhile, the pace of life at Beech Hill never slackened.

Carly had been helping Liz out all morning. They'd treated a kitten with fleas and an eye infection, a dog with an abscess on his foot and a cat that snored. Now, in the lull after surgery, Carly was visiting Hazel in intensive care.

The beagle was off her drip and taking water by mouth. Her sores had healed and the drug Paul Grey had chosen to fight against the tetanus condition was gradually taking effect. Slowly, little by little, Hazel was winning her battle for survival. But the dog still needed lots of physio to bring movement back to her stiff and wasted legs. Carly put her on the floor, knelt next to her and began work.

'This is to help you get back on your feet,' she explained, as she massaged the joints in the beagle's shoulders and hips. 'Mel says you have to try to stand at least four times a day. Do you think you can do it? Come on, try. See if you can stand up!'

Hazel responded to the sound of Carly's voice. She lifted her head from the floor and struggled to get her legs underneath her and scramble to her feet. But her legs slipped away weakly and she sank down.

'Good girl!' Carly praised the brave effort.

Determined, Hazel tried again. This time she got her legs under her, ready to take her weight for the first time since the lockjaw had taken hold.

'That's right! Try!' Carly urged. She concentrated so hard that she didn't turn round at the sound of the door opening quietly behind her.

The dog pushed with her legs. Slowly, with every bit of strength she could muster, she stood up.

'Good girl!' Carly breathed. She eased backwards two or three paces. 'Now, come to me!'

Hazel shook and swayed. She kept her eyes fixed on Carly. Trembling, lifting one stiff leg, she took her first step.

'Yes, you can do it!' Carly watched the beagle edge forwards, rocking awkwardly because of her stiff joints, shaking all over, but brave and determined. One step, two and then three. 'You're walking!' Carly cried, stretching out her arms and wrapping them round the exhausted dog.

Gently she picked Hazel up and carried her back to the warm, safe unit. She laid her down and turned to see that two other people had been watching the dog's moment of triumph.

'Well done!' Paul Grey stood by the door with a man Carly had never seen before. The man was short and well-built, with wavy brown hair and dark-rimmed glasses, dressed in a black leather jacket and jeans.

'Carly, this is Glen Pearson. He's come from the other side of town to take a look at our star patient here!' Carly's dad was smiling, ushering the stranger in, letting him study the beagle for a few seconds.

Who was Glen Pearson? Carly wondered. Another vet come to look at an unusual case? A student, perhaps? She turned to Paul Grey with a puzzled look.

'Bupinda contacted him,' her dad explained. 'She rang the Holybridge Green Cross vets and passed on our information about STR22.'

Carly let this sink in. She saw the man lean over the unit, watched as the beagle lifted her weary head and wagged her tail. Gently the man rested his hand on her head, his back towards them.

'Well?' Paul asked.

Carly held her breath, waiting for him to speak.

'Yes.' Glen Pearson nodded at last, his voice muffled. 'This is my dog. I've been looking everywhere for her. This is Heidi.'

The beagle had gone missing from home six weeks earlier. Glen Pearson told Carly and Paul Grey that the refuse collectors had called to empty the bins and left the garden gate open. Heidi must have seized her chance and sneaked out when Glen wasn't looking. Too late, he'd realised she'd gone walkabout and set off to scour the streets. By that time, perhaps an hour had gone by and there'd been no sign of his beloved dog.

'For days I was out there looking. I told the police and my vet at Holybridge, put cards in shop windows, an advert in the local paper. I refused to believe that Heidi could just vanish without a trace.'

'It must have been terrible.' Carly imagined the worry Glen must have gone through.

'I blamed myself, I blamed the binmen, I even blamed the police for not doing enough to help find Heidi.' He told them the full story over a cup of coffee in Paul's office. 'And I kept on expecting her to come back home of her own accord. I thought that one morning I would wake up and there she'd be, a bit battered and bruised maybe, but large as life.'

Paul nodded. 'It's a mystery how she ended up here. It's a long way from Holybridge, right across the city centre.'

'I don't expect we'll ever know.' Glen sighed. 'Maybe somebody spotted her on the loose and took her in, thinking she'd appreciate a nice new home.'

'Except that Hazel – I mean Heidi – must have been wearing a collar,' Carly cut in. She must get used to calling the beagle by her real name now. 'Wouldn't they read your address and phone number on the name-tag?'

'Hmm.' Glen was so relieved to have found Heidi that he couldn't give much thought to what might have happened.

'It's more likely that the person who spotted her thought they could make a bit of money out of pretending she was his own dog and trying to sell her,' Paul said. 'She's a nice pedigree animal, after all.'

Carly pictured how this plan might have backfired. The thief could have driven Heidi across the city to carry out his plan. But after that, Heidi could have seized her next chance to escape.

Lost in a strange part of town, wandering from street to street, she could have fallen in with a couple of stray dogs. And that, to cut a long story short, was probably how she'd come to join the pack of dogs running wild in Beech Hill. But, like Glen said, they would never know for sure.

'The important thing is, she's well and truly on the mend.' Paul stood up, pleased with the outcome. 'Thanks to the staff here, and to Carly. It's always the nursing that counts in a case like this.'

'And thanks to Hoody.' Carly reminded him that it had been Hoody who had discovered Heidi on the waste ground, and Hoody who had kept up the pressure for them to go on treating the very sick dog.

'Well, I hope to meet him soon, so I can tell him in person how grateful I am.' Glen Pearson stood up too. 'Now that I've found Heidi, I'll visit her every day until you say she's fit enough to come home.'

They left the office and crossed reception, shook hands and said goodbye. But, before she went to the kennels to get on with her chores, Carly glanced out to the carpark to see Hoody's older sister, Zoe, running towards the building. She flung open the door and rushed in.

'Paul, Hoody sent me! It's Vinny! You've got to come!' Zoe pleaded. Her face was pale, her short brown hair had flopped forward and clung to her damp forehead. She'd run a long way, so she was hot and out of breath.

'Where is he?' Immediately Carly's dad sized up the situation. He reached for his bag from under the reception desk.

'By Hillman's. That waste ground down the side.'

Carly felt her heart lurch. She grabbed Zoe's arm. 'What was he doing there? What happened?'

'Search me. I was shopping with Dean. We'd driven up with Hoody and Vinny, and parked the car on a bit of scrubland where the pub used to be and walked across to the supermarket. Hoody said something about checking the demolition site for some clues or other. Well, I never paid much attention, to be honest. Anyway, we did our shopping, and that's when we came out and found them.'

Hoody's sister stopped for breath. She pulled free from Carly and followed Paul Grey across the waiting area. 'The traffic's bad. It's quicker to go on foot!' she told him.

Carly's dad nodded. They set off running together up Beech Hill.

'So what's happened to Vinny?' Paul asked for as much information as he could gather before they reached the site.

'I don't know exactly. There was a crowd of people round him. I couldn't see.'

The knot of onlookers was still there. Carly spotted it ahead, bunched on the pavement under the giant billboards.

'I got him, Hoody!' Zoe cried as they drew level. She began to push through from the back towards the centre of the crowd. 'Watch out. Let the vet through!'

Reluctantly, the onlookers parted for Paul. Carly slipped through after him, catching a glimpse of Hoody crouched over a body lying still on the rough ground. She pushed the last two people aside for her first clear view.

Her dad was already on his knees beside Hoody. Zoe's boyfriend, Dean, stood behind them, warning people not to get too close. And then Carly saw Vinny lying motionless on his side, eyes closed, blood seeping from his torn mouth.

'How long's he been unconscious?' Paul Grey asked, kneeling to feel the dog's neck for a pulse.

'Ten minutes.' Hoody kept a blood-soaked scarf pressed hard against a gash on the dog's flank. 'I can't stop the bleeding!' he muttered. His face was grey, his unzipped jacket showed a T-shirt stained with blood.

'Right, we've got to get him back to Beech Hill as quickly as we can!' Paul decided.

'Is it safe to move him?' Carly fell to her knees beside Hoody and Vinny, wondering if Vinny could have broken bones or internal injuries as well as the cuts.

Her dad frowned. 'How did it happen? It wasn't a traffic accident, was it?'

'No. He was in a fight.' Hoody himself seemed to be struggling to breathe normally. His voice was strained. 'Another dog did this.'

'You should've seen it!' Someone in the crowd pushed forward to give his version. 'The dog was huge! It sank its teeth right in. This one never stood a chance!'

The elderly man made gestures to accompany his gory tale. But as Hoody gave way to Paul, who had begun to strap a dressing around Vinny's chest to stem the flow of blood, he sprang up to confront the story teller. 'That wasn't the dog that attacked Vinny, you idiot!' Angrily he pushed the man back and turned to Carly. 'It wasn't Merlin. He was the one who *stopped* the fight!'

Carly stared at Hoody's own scratched face and hands. He was shaking with shock and frustration. 'OK, I believe you. It was the grey dog, wasn't it?'

He nodded. 'It was my fault. I knew the pack would be hanging round here. I should've left Vin at home.'

Out of the corner of her eye, Carly could see her dad easing open the dog's bleeding mouth. 'Zoe said you were looking for clues!' she whispered. 'What clues?'

He glanced round the waste ground, at the oil-drums, the mounds of damp bricks and plaster. 'I don't know, do I? But I wanted to find out why Merlin brings the pack here. I wanted to find out what's so special about this place. All I needed was one clue!'

Carly sighed. 'Hoody, think about it!' She gestured towards the dismal piles of rubble. 'Maybe there is nothing special. No clues; nothing!'

'Then why? Why come here every day, like he's keeping watch ... waiting? Why here? Why the house by the canal?' He closed his eyes as if he was dizzy and trying to steady himself, then opened them quickly to concentrate on Vinny once more. 'How is he?' he asked Paul.

'His jaw's not broken. It looks like he bit his own tongue during the fight. There's one bad bite on his side.' He pointed to the white dressing which was already beginning to stain red. 'And other minor cuts all over his body. The problem is straightforward loss of blood.'

'It doesn't look as if he's gonna make it.' Someone in the crowd gave a gloomy opinion.

Others shook their heads and muttered that it was too late for the vet to do any good; Hoody should have picked Vinny up and run to the Rescue Centre with him instead of waiting on the spot where it had happened.

'Don't listen to them,' Paul advised. He pulled a roll of green canvas from his bag and laid it flat. 'You did the right thing. Pressing hard against the cut artery with your scarf has probably saved his life. Carly, we're going to lift Vinny on to the sheet. Ready?'

They slid their hands under the unconscious dog and lifted him smoothly, supporting his head, seeing his legs dangle limply as they placed him on the canvas. Carly wiped his mouth and folded a square of fresh dressing under it to catch the trickle of blood.

'Now, lift!' Paul told her.

Taking two corners each, they turned the sheet

of canvas into a makeshift stretcher. Dean stepped forward, parting the nosey crowd and making a way through for Paul and Carly.

'What will you do when we get back?' Carly wanted to know. She knew everyone in the street was stopping to look at them, asking questions and gossiping about the dogfight that had just taken place.

'We'll get him straight into surgery and stitch him up, then we'll give him a blood transfusion and hook him up on to a Hartmann's drip for the shock.' He described the emergency treatment that Vinny needed.

They crossed City Road at the traffic-lights, followed by Hoody, Zoe and Dean. Then they turned down Beech Hill, weaving between the Saturday shoppers, ignoring the stares.

As they ran down the hill and turned into the Rescue Centre, Carly noticed Vinny's eyes begin to flicker open. She heard him whimper and struggle to lift his head. 'He's coming round!' she warned.

'Is he in pain?' Hoody ran alongside.

Paul nodded. 'But we'll get him under

anaesthetic as soon as we can. Then he won't feel a thing.'

Inside the Centre, Liz and Mel were flicking through the appointment book and checking patient files. They saw the stretcher and sprang into action.

'Emergency admission!' Carly's father described what they needed to do. 'Scrub up and get ready for surgery. We'll take him straight through to the prep room.'

Inside the canvas sling, Vinny whined and writhed. Carly concentrated on getting him through reception. 'Wait here!' she told Hoody.

'Save him!' he whispered in a scared voice, standing helpless by the desk as they pushed through the swing-doors and carried Vinny into the shiny, brightly lit room. 'Save his life for me, please!'

8

Vinny lay on the operating table under a sterile sheet. Paul and Liz were at work, dressed in green theatre overalls and surgical gloves. Mel stood nearby, keeping her eye on the heart monitor and ready with extra anaesthetic if need be.

Carly watched them race to repair the deep gash in the dog's side. She tried not to think that it was Vinny under the sheet; not to picture him chasing sticks in the park, faithfully trotting along beside Hoody everywhere he went. She had to learn to be like her dad, able to put his personal feelings to one side while he worked.

All the same, she felt her mouth go dry and her whole body tremble as small clamps were inserted to prise the wound open. Then the vets could begin to sew the damaged artery and each layer of torn muscle. The clock on the wall ticked slowly, the bright lights glared.

'That's the last one.' Paul Grey watched Liz make the final suture in the bare skin surrounding the wound. Half an hour after the start of the operation, the assistant vet neatly snipped the final thread. 'How's he doing?' he asked Mel.

The nurse checked the monitors and the blood transfusion pack. 'Blood pressure's going up,' she confirmed.

'Good. But what are we going to do about the tear in his tongue?' Liz asked.

Paul lifted the sheet from Vinny's head. Carly scarcely recognised the lifeless face; head tilted back, tongue lolling. Her heart skipped a beat.

'We won't interfere with that,' her dad decided, inspecting it closely. 'It should heal by itself.'

'Does that mean you're through?' Mel rolled the emergency resuscitation trolley back against the wall.

Carly saw Vinny twitch and noticed the tip of his injured tongue curl to lick his top lip. She knew that this meant he was beginning to come round from the anaesthetic. 'Will he be OK?' She murmured the first words she'd spoken since surgery had begun.

Paul took a deep breath. He peeled off his gloves and nodded at Carly. 'So far, so good. Do you want to be the one to go and tell Hoody?'

'Come on, Vin, wake up!' Hoody sat by his dog in the recovery unit. He'd taken in the news that Vinny had got through the operation and now stood a good chance of recovery. But when Carly took him through to see him, he hadn't been able to hide his shock.

'It's OK, he'll come round in his own time,' Carly told him. The dog lay on his side. His eyes flickered open and shut, the scar looked vivid and ugly.

'Wake up, Vin!' Hoody whispered, not daring

to touch him. He crouched by his side. Tiny
nerves in his tense jaw clicked as he clung on to
the table. His own scuffed and cut face was white
with fear.

The dog's sides heaved in and out. His tongue
curled round his dry lips.

'He needs water!' Hoody told Carly.

Thinking fast, she went to the sink and drew
some fresh tap water into a dropper. The cool feel
of the water dripped on to Vinny's tongue would
help him come round, she knew. So she gave the
dropper to Hoody and watched again.

'Here, this is nice!' Hoody urged. Gently he let
the water trickle into the dog's mouth. 'Have a
drink. That's right, swallow it nice and slow.' He
stroked Vinny's throat to help him.

Vinny gulped and opened his eyes to gaze at
Hoody.

'See, you're gonna be OK!'

The dog wagged his tail. He licked his lips for
more water.

'You had a fight, right?' Hoody talked on, softly
stroking Vinny's head, leaning in close. 'This grey
dog jumped you from behind. You never stood a

chance. I tried to step in, but he turned on me too. Then you were on the ground and he was moving in for the kill.'

Carly listened to Hoody's description. She didn't try to interfere, but she would store this up for later: Hoody jabbering on to Vinny as if the dog understood every word. She allowed herself a secret smile.

'He could see you were bleeding, and it seemed to make him worse. You know, I really think he'd have finished you off if it hadn't been for Merlin!'

Vinny blinked. His breathing had grown deeper and more regular as he listened to the soothing sound of his owner's voice.

'You know Merlin? The big dog. He stepped right in between you and the grey dog, no messing. You should see him when he bares his teeth. It's awesome. A good job the grey dog thought so too. He wasn't arguing with the leader of the pack – no way!' Hoody went on talking, only glancing at Carly when he saw Vinny tuck his legs under him and try to sit up.

'It's OK.' She nodded. 'Let him try.'

So Hoody eased Vinny up, stroking him and telling him he was a good dog. 'You're tough, Vin. You'll get over it!'

Carly smiled. The anaesthetic had almost worn off, and Vinny was already looking more like himself. His head was up, his ears pricked, and his tail wagged slowly back and forth.

'And when you're better, we'll try again. All we need is one clue to trace Merlin's owner.' Hoody let Vinny know they weren't beaten yet. 'If they can do it for the beagle, we can do it for Merlin!'

'Carly!' Paul Grey spoke quietly from the doorway. He gestured for her to come out into the corridor.

She left Hoody and Vinny together. 'Thanks, Dad!' She wanted him to know she thought he was one of the best vets around.

'I'm glad it seems to be working out.' Paul walked her down the corridor towards reception. It was still only midday, and soon the waiting area would be filling up with more patients for afternoon surgery. 'But!' he said, stopping and turning to face her. It was in capital letters: 'BUT!'

Carly pulled a worried face. 'What have I done now?'

'Not you, Hoody. He obviously went looking for those stray dogs again. Didn't he listen to my "Leave it to Steve" message earlier in the week?'

'He was only trying to help.' Carly spoke up for him. 'You won't tell him off, will you?'

'No. He's been through enough already. But it does prove the point I was trying to make.' Pushing his hands deep into the pockets of his white coat, he made Carly meet his gaze. 'Messing with feral dogs is dangerous!'

She looked into his worried eyes and she nodded.

'Promise me you won't go looking for them by yourself, now that Hoody and Vinny are out of action for a while?'

Carly dropped her gaze. If she gave her word, it practically meant giving up on Merlin.

'I know you, Carly Grey.' Her dad was determined to pin her down. 'I can see your mind ticking over. You're probably planning a solo trip to that derelict house by the canal this very minute, now that Hoody's caught up here with Vinny!'

'Not exactly.' She hadn't thought that far.

'Well, then. Don't. You don't go anywhere near that flyover this weekend. OK?'

And give up on Merlin? She pleaded silently with her dark-brown eyes.

Paul's gaze didn't falter. 'Promise.'

'OK.' There was no avoiding it. She had to give her word.

For once during this damp, dreary autumn, the afternoon turned out sunny.

'Do you want to come out to the City Farm with me?' Steve asked, seeing Carly looking fed up in reception. 'I'm going over there to release two mallards I found trapped in plastic netting on the allotments.'

It was three o'clock. Hoody was still in the recovery unit with Vinny. Liz and Paul were working through a list of routine surgery: dental work on a ginger cat called Marmalade, and an operation to remove an air-gun pellet from the chest of a three-year-old female lurcher.

Carly had just phoned four more vets. She'd handed over details about Rosie, Oscar and, of course, Merlin, only to get the usual reply: 'No, sorry. No missing dogs on our list that fit those descriptions. But we'll keep a lookout for you.'

'No, thanks.' She sighed in answer to Steve's question. She crossed more names off her list, rested her chin in her hands, then watched the inspector take the two noisy birds out to the van.

'That's not like you.' Bupinda looked at her thoughtfully. 'Why not take a dog for a walk instead?'

Carly nodded. 'I guess I could take Oscar. He hasn't been out today.'

'Don't sound so enthusiastic!' The receptionist raised her eyebrows. 'Listen, do me a favour while you're out. You know the flower stall outside the supermarket? Can you buy me a bunch of yellow chrysanthemums if I give you the money?'

Carly agreed and went to fetch the boisterous terrier-cross. Oscar jumped and barked at the sight of the lead. His glee cheered Carly up. By the time she'd looked in on Hoody and Vinny, taken the flower money from Bupinda and got out into the afternoon sun, she was in a better mood.

'Hi there. How's the brown dog?' A passer-by on Beech Hill recognised Carly from the emergency dash to save Vinny.

'Fine, thanks.' She smiled back. Eager Oscar tugged at the lead. He went one way round a lamppost while she went the other. 'Oops!' Disentangling themselves, they went on their way towards City Road.

An old silver car drew up at the kerb. Hoody's sister, Zoe, wound down the passenger-side window. 'Is Hoody still at your place?' she asked Carly.

Carly picked Oscar up to stop him from winding his lead around another lamppost. 'Yep. But don't worry, Vinny's much better!'

Zoe nodded. 'Thank heavens for that. If Hoody had lost Vin, I don't know what we'd have done. He thinks the world of that dog!' Like her brother, Zoe came across as tough. But she too was soft-hearted. 'Tell your dad thanks from me!' she called, as Dean revved the worn engine and chugged on down the road.

'Come on, Oscar, or we'll never get to that flower stall!' Carly put him down and they set off again, across the pedestrian crossing and along the crowded pavement towards Hillman's.

A bank of bright flowers came into view: yellow, orange and red autumn colours. Carly switched the dog's lead from one hand to the other to search for the money in her jacket pocket.

Oscar must have felt the lead slacken. He tugged hard.

'Hey!' Carly called the cheeky dog back. The lead had slipped from her hand and he was trailing it along after him as he nipped between the legs of shoppers on the pavement. 'Oscar, come back!'

The little white dog ignored her. Tail up, looking straight ahead, he broke into a trot.

'Come back!' Carly wove through the crowd, past the flower stall. She lost sight of Oscar, then spotted him again, scooting along the length of the supermarket, close into the plate-glass frontage. He swerved past a parked bicycle, still trailing his lead, ignoring her shouts.

'Stop that dog!' A man standing on the corner tried to help. He'd seen Oscar nip by and heard Carly call.

Too late, the cheeky mongrel slipped by a bus queue and disappeared amongst the trolleys in the trolley park beside the supermarket.

'Where's he off to in such a hurry?' A woman in the bus queue grinned at Carly as she rushed to follow the runaway.

But this wasn't funny. She had no time to reply. Whereas Oscar had been small enough to weave in and out of the metal trolleys, Carly had to make a detour and go round. It gave him chance to dash further ahead. She caught a flash of white across the supermarket carpark, saw the tall advertising billboards beyond.

'Oh, no!' She put on speed. Now she knew where Oscar was headed. Like it or not, she would have to follow him.

I only promised Dad I wouldn't go near the canal again! she told herself.

Yes, but you know what he meant, a second voice inside her head told her as she wove through the parked cars. *He meant don't go anywhere*

where the wild dogs are likely to be!

But he said the canal! She tried to convince herself that she wasn't breaking her promise. *Anyway, it's the afternoon. The dogs won't be here!*

Silence. Her conscience refused to argue the point.

What am I supposed to do? Exasperated, Carly protested to herself. *I can't just let Oscar run off!*

Here they were, on the edge of the rough ground where Vinny had had his fight, the wasteland haunted by the notorious pack of dogs. Oscar was forging ahead, through the tall pink weeds growing between cracks in the concrete, over mounds of bricks and out of sight.

Carly closed her eyes. 'Dad will understand!' she said out loud.

Clenching her fists, calling the dog's name, she set out across the demolition site.

9

'The gang's not here! Oscar, come back!' Carly stumbled up a pile of bricks to call the runaway.

The dog sniffed excitedly round the base of the oil-drums where she and Steve had found the iguana. He was obviously looking for dogs from his old pack, recognising recent scents.

A woman parking a four-wheel drive on the edge of the waste ground gave Carly a curious look.

Oscar trailed his lead after him, sniffing here and there. Then he scratched at the surface of a patch of mud, sniffed again, trotted on.

Carly jumped down from the mound. Calling him was no good, she realised. She would have to catch up with him and snatch the lead instead.

So she ran quietly towards the drums, hoping to come close without Oscar noticing. Once she was within reach, she planned to step smartly on to his trailing lead and trap him.

The dog poked at the weeds growing round the base of the drums with his wet, black nose, enjoying the smells. He cocked his head to one side.

'What have you heard now?' Carly muttered. She was tiptoeing towards him, but was still ten metres away when Oscar started to listen, pricked his pointed ears, then disappeared eagerly round the back of the stack of rusty drums.

She soon found out. There was a low growl, and a sudden, surprised yap from Oscar. The growl turned to a snarl. Carly broke into a run across the rubble-strewn ground and rounded the corner.

It was the grey dog glaring down from the top

of another mound, teeth bared. He was alone. Had he been turfed out by Merlin and the rest of the pack after his vicious fight with Vinny earlier that morning? Carly could only guess as she stared at him and saw his long, matted hair sweep the filthy ground. He crouched, ready to leap.

'Watch out!' She yelled an unnecessary warning at Oscar. The small white dog was already backing off, tail between his legs.

The German shepherd-cross edged forward. One glaring eye was brown, the other a strange, whitish-grey. The hair on his neck was raised in a ferocious ruff.

This is the dog that nearly killed Vinny! Carly thought. *And Vinny's bigger and tougher than Oscar by far*. Holding her breath, rooted to the spot, she wondered how to step in and save the frightened mongrel.

Luckily, Oscar could think for himself. He wasn't strong, but he was quick, and there was no disgrace in running away from an enemy as fierce as the savage grey dog. In a flash, he turned and shot away over the uneven ground.

The renegade stray made his leap from the mound. Too late. Oscar was darting between scrubby bushes, back the way he had come.

But the grey dog was running now. His long legs carried him swiftly, faster than Carly could follow. Soon he would overtake the fleeing Oscar.

Oscar must have heard the feet pounding after him. He darted sideways, up a mound of rubble and planks of rotting wood, leaping down the far side.

Carly changed direction, trying to cut across and come between the two dogs. Her heart thumped, she knew she too was running into danger, so she stooped and seized a short wooden pole, then ran on.

The grey dog outran her. He was almost on top of Oscar when she heard the car engine and saw the big four-wheel drive. It hadn't parked after all. The woman driver must have spotted the dogs and worked out what was happening. Now she roared her engine and came bumping and rocking over the waste ground, straight at them. The two dogs veered off to the side, running from the common enemy.

Carly stared, terrified that the dogs would be too slow to get out of the way. Did the woman really mean to run them over? The wide wheels and sturdy bull bar careered towards them.

They reached the stack of oil-drums only two or three metres ahead of the car. She saw Oscar peel off to the right, the grey dog to the left. The driver wrenched at the steering wheel and pulled the car to the left. She kept at the attacker, giving Oscar a chance to curve back towards Carly and come running to the safety of her arms.

Carly dropped the pole and swept the little dog up. He panted and gasped, his ribcage heaving in and out.

The car kept on after the grey dog, running him off the waste ground into a big timberyard beyond. The dog reached it, still fleeing, for once feeling what it was like for the hunter to be hunted.

Carly wasn't sorry for the fierce dog to be taught a lesson. She watched the driver of the car chase him to the limit of the waste ground, saw him squeeze through a gap in the broken fencing, scared but uninjured. He ran on, down a long lane of stored timber and finally out of sight.

The car braked and turned. Slowly the driver picked her way between piles of rubble and broken concrete towards the spot where Carly and Oscar stood.

As she stopped the car and got out, Carly calmed Oscar. She stroked him and spoke softly to him, wondering who his rescuer could be.

The woman was medium height and plump, with dyed dark-brown hair and bright red lipstick. She was smartly dressed in a fitted black jacket and trousers. 'That soon showed him!' she said with a satisfied smile.

'Thanks!' Carly put a shaky Oscar down on to the ground.

The woman went on smiling. 'I saw what was going on when I came to park my car to go to Hillman's. It didn't look like a fair contest to me, and I couldn't just stand by and watch the poor little chap get torn to shreds.'

'Do you like dogs?' Carly warmed to the woman for what she'd done and for the friendly, down-to-earth way in which she spoke.

She nodded. 'I've got two of my own. Black Labradors. If I'd had them with me today, they could've taken your side and evened things up a bit!'

'Where are they?' Carly kept an anxious eye on Oscar, who was keeping a lookout in case the grey dog came back.

'At home. We live out of town now, but as a matter of fact this would have been home turf for Buster and Buttons. This is where we used to live!' She gestured towards the heaps of demolished bricks and rubble.

'Right here?' Carly could hardly remember the buildings that had once stood on the site. 'Wasn't it a row of shops?'

'Yes, and a pub,' the woman reminded her. 'The Rose and Crown. I'm Lisa Shaw. I used to be the landlady here.' She looked sadly at the expanse of wasteland. 'I still come back here to the supermarket to do my shopping. The countryside is nice, but to be honest I do miss the old place!'

'So you must have known the other people who lived here?' Carly saw in a flash that Lisa

Shaw could be the answer to her prayers. Not only had she saved Oscar, but she might be able to provide the vital clue about Merlin. 'Do you remember if anyone owned a giant dog? This big . . . pale fawn colour . . . like a Great Dane?'

'Hang on!' The ex-landlady smiled as the words tumbled out of Carly's mouth. 'Yes, you must mean Neil Somers. He worked for me as a barman for about six months, just before we closed down. He used to bring Shadow to work with him sometimes: a lovely, gentle creature, he was. My two dogs loved him.'

'Shadow!' Carly whispered Merlin's real name. 'So he would know this area well?'

Lisa Shaw nodded. 'Neil used to leave him in the yard at the back of the pub, which would be somewhere near where that stack of oil-drums is now. Shadow was a terrific guard dog because of his size, but in reality he wouldn't harm a fly.'

This must *be the same dog!* There was absolutely no doubt. Carly held her breath as Mrs Shaw talked on. *Now for the crucial question*: 'Do you know where Neil Somers lives now?'

'Let's see. He used to live in a flat in a big old

house by the canal; I know that much.'

'It's all closed up,' Carly jumped in quickly.

'Ah well, he must have moved on, then.'

'Do you know where to?' She willed Lisa Shaw to say yes.

The ex-landlady frowned, then shrugged. 'I'm afraid not. The Rose and Crown belonged to a big brewery with pubs all over the country. I seem to remember that Neil's idea was to get another bar job with the same brewery. What was it exactly? That's right; he might even have been planning to get them to train him as a landlord so he could run his own pub. But I don't know if it ever came to anything.'

'You lost touch with him and Shadow?' Carly knew that her face must show how disappointed she felt. After the sudden high of identifying the dog's owner, it was like being dumped into a deep, dark pit.

Mrs Shaw sighed. 'Neil was a bit of a drifter, really. Don't get me wrong; he was a reliable worker and he loved that dog of his to bits. But he had no roots that I ever heard of. His parents were both dead, he didn't seem to have any brothers and sisters. And I somehow doubt that he ever carried out his plan to train as a landlord. Why are you asking? Is it Neil or his dog you're so interested in?'

'Both,' Carly assured her. She'd soaked up every scrap of information. 'Did Neil have any friends who might have his new address?'

'Not that I know of. If he did, they've probably moved on themselves by now. The pub was the main meeting place round here and, since they pulled it down more than a year ago, people have gone their separate ways.' Lisa Shaw gave Carly a sympathetic shrug. She turned and gazed across the demolition site, as Oscar rooted happily once more amongst the litter and the rubble.

'That's city life for you,' she said sadly. 'People move on. You lose touch. It's the way it goes.'

'Vinny, you're a star!' Hoody hadn't left his dog's side for a single second since the fight with the grey mongrel. He stayed all Saturday afternoon, talking to him and willing him to get better. 'Look at him, Carly! He's still a bit groggy, but he's standing up already.'

Carly was almost as pleased and relieved as Hoody. Apart from the bare patch of skin and the fresh scar, no one would have guessed that only hours earlier Vinny had been at death's door. 'Here's something to eat.' She handed Hoody a sandwich that she'd brought to the resuscitation unit from the flat.

He took it and ate hungrily, not once taking his eyes off Vinny. 'See, he's looking better, isn't he?' he mumbled between mouthfuls.

'Loads better.'

'Because you're a star, that's why,' Hoody told him. 'You're not gonna let some sneaky dog jump you from behind and finish you off, are you?'

' "Woof-woof, grr-woof!" ' Carly mimicked the dog's answer. 'That means "No way!" ' she laughed.

'Ha-ha!' Hoody blushed. 'OK, so it serves me right.'

'You're the one who told me it was crazy to talk to an animal as if they could understand,' she agreed. Then she went on with what she'd come down to talk to him about in the first place. 'We have a name, but no address, no other leads.' She told him every detail she'd learned about Neil Somers and Shadow. 'So near, yet so far from being able to find his owner!' She sighed.

'It means we were right about him going back to hang round the places he knew best,' Hoody reminded her.

'And right about him not being vicious.' To Carly this was important. 'Mrs Shaw says he's a lovely, gentle dog.'

'He saved Vinny,' Hoody said. 'I'll never forget that.'

Carly watched Vinny take a few groggy steps towards them. She thought of Shadow's brave and kind heart. He deserved better than a life scavenging for food amongst derelict buildings. But she also knew that he was a free spirit and should never be cooped up in a kennel at Beech Hill, hoping against hope that someone would give him a new home. What she wanted for Shadow was justice.

'If only we could pay him back and save him in return.' She sighed again.

*

'Heidi is making exceptionally good progress,' Paul Grey told Glen Pearson next morning, as Carly stood at the door of the intensive care unit, looking on.

The beagle's owner had kept his promise to visit whenever he could. Today, Sunday, was his day off from his job as a salesman at a big car showroom in the city centre, and he planned to spend it all with Heidi.

'We'll keep her in until we've completed her course of treatment, but it's safe to say that she really is out of danger and on the mend.'

Mr Pearson had been learning how to massage Heidi's stiff limbs so that she could walk and build up her strength. Now the dog was doing her best to stand and totter towards him.

Carly could see that her dad was happy to confirm the good news. He backed out of the room and led her to the kennels, where Vinny had spent the night.

But before they went in, he stopped. 'We should get in touch with Hoody and tell him Vinny can go home later today.'

'No need.' Carly opened the door to a chorus

131

of barks. 'He's already been here for over an hour!'

Hoody had arrived very first thing. In fact, it had been hard to persuade him to go home at all the night before. Only when Vinny had fallen sound asleep had her friend reluctantly agreed to go back to Beacon Street. And he'd been waiting on the front step at half past seven when Carly had come down to feed the dogs.

'What do you want now?' Hoody hardly gave them a chance to step inside before he bit their heads off with a suspicious question.

Paul grinned and went straight to Vinny's kennel. 'Nothing. This is a routine round, that's all. Vin looks perky enough this morning.'

'When can he come home?'

'Later today,' Paul confirmed.

'Great!' Hoody spun back to tell Vinny. 'You hear that? You don't have to stay here by yourself tonight . . .'

Above the row of the barking dogs, while Hoody was chatting away to Vinny, Carly heard Steve's voice call from reception.

'Hi. Where is everyone?'

She cut back along the corridor to find the inspector looking serious.

'RTA,' he told her abruptly. 'A dog's been in an accident with a bus on City Road. He was roaming loose, criss-crossing the main road like a crazy thing. He ran straight under the wheels of the bus, the driver never stood a chance. They rang me to go and pick up the body.'

'Was he killed outright?' Carly glanced out at the inspector's van.

'Yep. That's one good thing. He didn't suffer.'

'Do you need to make a phone call?' She knew the routine would be to contact the dog's owners to tell them what had happened.

But Steve shook his head. 'Not this time. It's a stray from the local pack.'

She gasped. 'Which one?'

'The one that had the fight with Vinny.'

She pictured the lean, long-haired grey dog, the hungry jaws and wild, odd-coloured eyes.

'One less stray to bring in,' Steve said flatly. He took a form from the rack behind Bupinda's desk and began to fill it out. 'And no more fights for him from now on.'

As Steve filled in the details, Carly felt confused. Perhaps it was for the best: the grey dog had been a danger to everyone and everything that crossed his path. But it could hardly have been his fault. Once upon a time even this most savage dog must have been a helpless puppy needing a good home and kind people to look after him.

If anyone was to blame, it was the person who'd taken him in then let him down. She thought long and hard about the fierce stray's lonely, neglected life.

'Anyway,' Steve went on, 'after I've finished here, I'm going to take one more shot at bringing in the leader of the pack; your precious Merlin.'

'His name's Shadow.' Carly brought him up to date with what she'd learned from Lisa Shaw.

'That suits him.' Steve gave the first faint smile since he'd arrived. 'He flits silently here and there, and you have to admit that it's hard to pin him down.'

'The dog that can't be captured.' She smiled back.

'Until today!' Steve promised. 'Today is going

to be the day, I can feel it!' He said it would be five minutes before he was ready to set off. 'Do you fancy coming along?'

'I do and I don't.' With her feelings about Shadow as mixed as they were, and recalling Hoody's forecast that bringing him in would be a death sentence, Carly knew it wasn't as simple as Steve made it sound.

'Well, make up your mind.' He gave her a long, questioning look. 'Meet me here if you decide you want to come.'

10

The inspector hurried outside to the van, while Carly went back to the kennels to try and get Hoody's advice. 'I think I'd better go,' she told him. 'Only, I don't know if I can bear to see Shadow cornered. What would you do if you were me?'

Hoody shrugged. 'Dunno. Leave me out of it. I'm staying here with Vin.'

The dog wagged his tail and nudged Hoody's hand with his head. The boy crouched down to stroke him.

'Thanks a lot.' She sighed. 'Maybe I won't go either.'

Hoody shrugged again. This time he said nothing.

'You think I ought to go?'

Silence.

'Do you think it'd be better for one of us two to be there?' *Speak to me*! she urged. *Give me a clue about what you're thinking!*

Silence.

'You do, don't you? If it has to happen, at least I could tell Shadow not to worry, that we're not trying to harm him!' Carly willed Hoody to help her make up her mind. At this rate, Steve would already have left.

'OK, I'm off!' She dashed to the door, then stopped. 'If only we could find out more about this Neil Somers!'

'How?' Suddenly, Hoody was more interested. He turned towards her.

'I don't know, do I?' Exasperated, she pushed the door, saw Steve heading down the corridor towards reception. 'OK, let's see. What do we know already? He used to live with Shadow by

137

the canal. He worked at the Rose and Crown. He wanted to carry on working for the same brewery ... Hey, that's it!'

'*What's* it?'

'The brewery! Don't you see: that's our new lead!'

Slowly Hoody's puzzled frown cleared. 'Yeah!'

Carly came quickly back into the room. She crouched beside him, stroking Vinny absent-mindedly as she spoke. 'Listen, Hoody. I'll go with Steve and make sure we bring Shadow in safe and sound. You know what you have to do while we're out?'

Hoody nodded. 'Ring the brewery, see if they've got Neil Somers' new address.'

'Right!' She jumped up and ran to catch up with Steve. 'That's how we're going to get in touch with him. Through the brewery; OK!'

She ignored Hoody's warning as she sped down the corridor.

'I'll try, but they probably won't know any more than that ex-landlady you bumped into!' he called after her. 'Whatever you do, don't hold your breath!'

*

'This is going to be even harder than I thought!' Steve told Carly. He pulled the van on to a patch of gravel next to the gardeners' brick-built store in Beech Hill Park.

For over an hour they'd cruised the streets looking for signs of the pack of stray dogs. They'd begun on the waste ground near the supermarket, expecting Shadow to lead the dogs along their usual morning route, but they'd waited there for half an hour in vain. Then they'd driven slowly along City Road, asking passers-by if they'd seen the pack. 'No' came the answer several times, until a teenage boy on a bike at a set of red traffic-lights told them 'Yes'.

'Where?' Carly had felt the boy staring suspiciously into the van at Steve's uniform.

'In the park.' He'd smirked, watched the lights change to green, and ridden off.

Should they believe him? 'It's not normal for Shadow to take them to the park in the morning,' she'd pointed out.

But Steve had said it wasn't a normal morning. Perhaps the pack had witnessed the grey dog's fatal accident and run off in panic. He'd thought it was worth following the boy's tip-off, and so here they were in the park.

They scanned the green slopes, the swings and roundabouts, the long stretch of grey water surrounded by bushes and trees. There was plenty of activity in the park: people pushing push-chairs, children playing in the playground, but no sign of the dogs. Now even Steve wasn't sure.

'It's weird,' he confessed. 'As if the dogs know we're trying to track them down and they're keeping well out of sight.'

Carly frowned. 'Maybe they did see the grey dog get killed,' she said slowly. 'And if they panicked like you said, maybe they split up in different directions.'

'So where would they choose to gather together again?' Steve asked, gazing out of the van at the busy scene. 'Obviously not the park!'

'Somewhere quiet,' Carly suggested. 'Somewhere they all know well.'

Steve gave her time to think. 'It's guesswork,' he admitted. 'But it's all we've got to go on.'

'It would have to be a place where they all feel safe.' She pictured another stretch of cold, grey water. But this one was man-made and flanked by tall warehouses. A flyover carried fast traffic overhead and an old house stood in its shadow, its windows boarded, its iron railings rusting in the wind and rain.

'The canal!' she told Steve, certain this time that this was where they would finally track down the elusive Shadow.

The first dog they saw came trotting along the side of the canal. She was a small white and black terrier type, a bit like Oscar, and she was alone.

'Keep back!' Carly hissed at Steve.

They pressed themselves against the concrete support for the flyover, staying deep in the shadows. The eager dog ignored them and headed for the old house.

'Looks like you were right!' Steve whispered to Carly.

The dog squeezed through the railings into the overgrown garden. A second one appeared from round the back of the building, and then a third, wary at first, then greeting the newcomer with wagging tails.

'So where's Shadow?' Carly crept nearer, aware of the traffic rumbling overhead, of the high walls to every side that dwarfed the deserted house.

'Wait.' He watched more dogs coming and going along the canal-side. They seemed to follow the same path into the house: through the gap in the railings, across the garden into the yard, then in through an unseen entrance at the back.

'Should we take a look inside?' After ten minutes Carly had watched half a dozen different dogs use the route. It was beginning to seem strange that so far there had been no sign of Shadow.

Steve checked the rope and muzzle he'd brought from the van. He nodded. 'But go carefully!'

They crept forward to the gap in the railings. Would the dogs spot them and drive them away?

'Me first,' Steve insisted, easing himself through the railings. 'It's like entering the lion's den!' he joked nervously, indicating that Carly could follow him into the garden.

Two dogs came out of the dark house. They were thin and covered in sores, cringing past the intruders, tails down. Carly watched them slide by and escape through the gap. The poor creatures were obviously too weak and frightened to challenge them. She gathered her courage and went in after the inspector.

Steve rounded the corner into the yard. 'Here's where they get in and out of the house.' He pointed to a broken cellar door down some steep stone steps. The door hung from one hinge. It creaked as it swung to and fro.

From inside the dismal building, at ground level, they heard a high, yapping bark and the scrabbling of claws against bare floorboards.

'That's not Shadow!' Carly muttered.

'No, but there's definitely at least one more dog in there,' Steve said, going ahead down the cellar steps.

Inside the badly lit basement it was too dark to see. They could still hear the yapping and scratching above their heads, so Steve turned on a torch and flashed the yellow beam around the grimy whitewashed walls, looking for steps up to the ground floor.

The torch beam picked out old wooden ladders toppled across the dirty stone floor, coils of frayed rope, a box of oily tools.

'Over there!' Carly saw the way out up some narrow stone steps. She ran across, steadied herself against the damp wall, then took the worn, uneven steps two at a time. Steve followed close behind.

At the top of the steps there was a closed door.

'It must have slammed shut in the wind,' Steve guessed. 'If this is the dogs' only way in and out of the actual house, whatever's behind here must have got themselves trapped!' He ran the torch beam up and down the sturdy door.

'For goodness knows how long!' Carly added. Did this explain why the pack had scattered and why Shadow hadn't been seen for more than twenty-four hours?

Steve saw that there was no handle on the cellar side of the door, so Carly stood to one side as he put his shoulder to the door and shoved.

There was the sound of splintering wood. The lock broke and the door flew open.

They burst out of the cellar into a long, dusty hallway and came face to face with a frantic, small, dark-brown dog.

'What's all the noise?' Steve said kindly, bending down to pick her up.

The dog yapped and ducked. She darted between Steve's legs, past Carly and down the cellar steps.

But Carly hardly took any notice. She was staring along the hallway, up a flight of broad stairs with ornate, carved banisters. There was a huge creature standing quietly on the landing, gazing down at them. He was caught in a shaft of weak daylight that filtered through the filthy landing window. She could see his smooth, pale coat, his massive head, his ever-watchful, amber eyes.

'Shadow!' Carly said softly.

The dog heard his own name for the first time in who knew how long? He seemed to sigh and drop his head, then turned for a last look out of the window. He gazed out across the overgrown garden, to the canal and the tower blocks beyond. But no – the one person he was always waiting for was nowhere to be seen.

Steve mounted the bottom step with the muzzle raised in both hands, but Carly touched his arm to stop him. She knew there wasn't going to be a struggle.

'Come here, Shadow. There's a good boy!'

She hardly needed to raise her voice above a whisper before the giant dog turned from the window, his long vigil at an end. Slowly he came down the stairs and gave himself up at last.

'He looks so sad!' Carly whispered as they drove Shadow back to Beech Hill.

She kept looking over her shoulder at the defeated dog. He lay quiet in the back of the van, his heavy head resting on his front paws, his eyes fixed on Carly.

'There was no fight left in him,' Steve agreed. He'd been surprised at how easily the dog had given himself up and let himself be led to the van parked by the canal.

'It's as if he knew there was no point waiting

any longer for his owner to show up.' She felt tears prick her eyes. 'Like, suddenly he gave up.'

She'd whispered his name and the light had gone out of his eyes. At that moment hope had died.

And what now for the dog that ran wild? A narrow kennel at the Rescue Centre, a blue card and a number: STR26. Carly swallowed hard and looked away from Shadow as the van turned into Beech Hill.

Her dad was waiting for them at the door. He watched Steve get out of the van and unlock the back door, and saw Carly reach inside to coax the stray dog out.

'Come on, Shadow, we won't harm you!' she whispered. But she could hardly meet the dog's blank gaze.

Slowly, awkwardly, Shadow got to his feet. He hung his giant head as he stepped from the van.

As she helped him down, Carly heard a strange sound from behind: *tap-tap*, like a walking stick or a crutch. She felt Shadow stiffen and look up. The light that had gone from his eyes when she'd first whispered his name suddenly came back.

'It's me, Shadow!' A man's voice broke the silence. 'Come here, boy. Come and say hello!'

The dog brushed Carly aside. Ears pricked, head high, he surged across the carpark.

The man leaned on his crutch. He was pale and thin, with dark hair down to his shoulders. Reaching out a shaky hand to Shadow, Neil Somers greeted his long-lost dog.

'Thanks to Hoody!' Paul Grey reported, taking everyone inside to explain how the reunion had come about. 'He's the one who rang the brewery who used to employ Neil at the Rose and Crown. They told Hoody that they had trained Neil to take over his own pub. They had recently found a place for him and Shadow in a town thirty kilometres south of here.

'But they'd only been in the new pub a couple of weeks when there was a late-night break-in. The thieves kept Shadow quiet by coshing him over the head. Then they stole the cash from the till and finished off the job by dealing with Neil in the same way as they'd dealt with Shadow.'

'I could have died,' Neil confirmed. 'They left me unconscious. A neighbour found me and called 999. He didn't think about Shadow until the ambulance arrived and took me off to hospital. Then he realised there was no dog around. The thieves must have bundled him into their getaway car thinking that if they left him behind he would soon come round and raise the alarm. It was either that or kill him, and the thieves weren't that cruel, thank heavens.' He kept his arm firmly round the dog's neck as they sat in reception, working out what had happened.

'And that was the last you saw of Shadow until now?' Carly asked.

Neil Somers nodded. 'It was three weeks back. I've been in hospital ever since. That's where Hoody tracked me down earlier this morning. For a while they didn't know if I would be able to walk again. And, to be honest, I couldn't help thinking the worst about Shadow.' His voice faltered and he held on even tighter.

'The police eventually traced the getaway car

back to the city, but by that time there was no sign of any dog. Shadow seemed to have vanished into thin air, and I really thought the burglars must have finished him off for good after they'd driven him away.'

'Easier said than done.' Paul smiled. 'He obviously gave them the slip, but couldn't find his way out of the city to the new pub that you'd moved to. So he came back to the places he knew: namely, the house by the canal where you and he used to live and the site of the old Rose and Crown.'

'And he found there was nothing left of the old pub!' Carly whispered. 'Just an empty shell and a pile of rubble.'

'He waited for you anyway!' Hoody spoke up. He had Vinny at his side and a look of triumph on his face. 'For three whole weeks. He never gave in!'

Neil Somers stood up and managed a smile. He gazed fondly at his faithful dog. 'Shadow always was an amazing dog,' he said proudly.

Carly beamed at Hoody, but said nothing. She was too happy to speak.

No doubt Neil Somers would have to go back to hospital until he was completely better. In the meantime, Shadow would stay at Beech Hill. There would be walks in the park, weekend trips out to the countryside . . .

'And in case you think it's all over,' Paul Grey broke into her daydream, 'there's a kennel full of dogs all begging for exercise!' He began a list of routine chores that went on and on.

'And homes to be found for Oscar and Rosie,' Carly agreed. She went to fetch the terrier-cross from the kennels. 'Maybe not today, but soon,' she promised him, as she and Hoody left her dad and Neil Somers busily making arrangements for Shadow.

Gleeful Oscar led her, Hoody and Vinny to the busy park. He scuttled ahead along the avenue of tall trees down towards the lake, chasing the fallen leaves and yelping for joy.

Somewhere out there must be the right owner for the bouncy little dog. 'A really nice home with a big garden where you can play!' Carly murmured, staring after the small white dot in the distance. 'Don't worry, tomorrow we'll find you that perfect person!'

Dreaming again, ignoring Hoody's disgruntled 'Huh!', Carly shoved her cold hands deep into her pockets and walked on.

ANIMAL ALERT SERIES
Jenny Oldfield

All Hodder Children's books are available at your local bookshop, or can be ordered direct from the publisher. Just tick the titles you would like and complete the details below. Prices and availability are subject to change without prior notice.

Please enclose a cheque or postal order made payable to *Bookpoint Ltd*, and send to: Hodder Children's Books, 39 Milton Park, Abingdon, OXON OX14 4TD, UK. Email Address: orders@bookpoint.co.uk

If you would prefer to pay by credit card, our call centre team would be delighted to take your order by telephone. Our direct line *01235 400414* (lines open 9.00 am–6.00 pm Monday to Saturday, 24 hour message answering service). Alternatively you can send a fax on *01235 400454*.

TITLE		FIRST NAME		SURNAME	

ADDRESS	
DAYTIME TEL:		POST CODE	

If you would prefer to pay by credit card, please complete:
Please debit my Visa/Access/Diner's Card/American Express (delete as applicable) card no:

Signature .... Expiry Date: ....

If you would NOT like to receive further information on our products please tick the box. ❏

HOME FARM TWINS
Jenny Oldfield

66127 5	Speckle The Stray	£3.50	❏
66128 3	Sinbad The Runaway	£3.50	❏
66129 1	Solo The Homeless	£3.50	❏
66130 5	Susie The Orphan	£3.50	❏
66131 3	Spike The Tramp	£3.50	❏
66132 1	Snip and Snap The Truants	£3.50	❏
68990 0	Sunny The Hero	£3.50	❏
68991 9	Socks The Survivor	£3.50	❏
68992 7	Stevie The Rebel	£3.50	❏
68993 5	Samson The Giant	£3.50	❏
69983 3	Sultan The Patient	£3.50	❏
69984 1	Sorrel The Substitute	£3.50	❏
69985 X	Skye The Champion	£3.50	❏
69986 8	Sugar and Spice The Pickpockets	£3.50	❏
69987 6	Sophie The Show-off	£3.50	❏

All Hodder Children's books are available at your local bookshop, or can be ordered direct from the publisher. Just tick the titles you would like and complete the details below. Prices and availability are subject to change without prior notice.

Please enclose a cheque or postal order made payable to *Bookpoint Ltd*, and send to: Hodder Children's Books, 39 Milton Park, Abingdon, OXON OX14 4TD, UK. Email Address: orders@bookpoint.co.uk

If you would prefer to pay by credit card, our call centre team would be delighted to take your order by telephone. Our direct line *01235 400414* (lines open 9.00 am–6.00 pm Monday to Saturday, 24 hour message answering service). Alternatively you can send a fax on *01235 400454*.

TITLE		FIRST NAME		SURNAME	

ADDRESS	

DAYTIME TEL:		POST CODE	

If you would prefer to pay by credit card, please complete:
Please debit my Visa/Access/Diner's Card/American Express (delete as applicable) card no:

Signature .... Expiry Date: ....

If you would NOT like to receive further information on our products please tick the box. ❏